Lost
Angels

BRIAN COLBORNE

- 1 -

The driver shook his head to stave off the heaviness of his eyelids. He opened them wide and blinked in rapid succession, yet another attempt to keep himself from drifting off to sleep behind the wheel. He looked over at his sleeping wife and wished he was in her place. A quick glance in the mirror showed his little girl hunched over in her booster seat; a glinting string of drool stuck to her lower lip and forearm.

The dark, open road waged its war on his alertness and, at last, he was forced to admit defeat. He slowed the car and pulled over on the shoulder. The gravel crunched under the tires and his wife stirred. She stretched her legs out in front of herself and yawned. With a tilt of her dreary head, she looked at him through bleary eyes.

"Everything okay?"

"Yeah, but I need to tag you in. Just for an hour or two."

She smiled and nodded as she unbuckled her seatbelt. They both got out and met at the front of the car. He stopped to put his arms around her waist and gave her a kiss to thank her for waking up. His hands moved up and down her back and he pulled her closer. She pushed away and playfully slapped his arm as she stepped around him.

"If you get yourself all excited, you won't be able to sleep." He smiled at her with his hands held up in surrender and headed to the passenger side. They both eased into the car and she touched his cheek as he settled in his seat. As she reached for the gear shift, he saw her eyes widen and she let out a shriek. Startled, he straightened up in his seat. There, standing in the harsh beams of the headlights, were two young girls. The taller one reached her hands out toward the hood of the car. Frozen in shock and terror, he stared out. She shuffled her bare feet closer. Her dry, cracked lips opened as she neared. Behind her, the shorter one slit her eyes against the light and crumbled to the ground. They wore tattered rags. Their hair was unkempt and matted in knotty nests. His wife had her mouth covered and breathed sharp bursts of air through her nostrils. The tall girl stretched her fingers out and placed her bony hand on the hood, leaning against it. She looked up at them, the light no longer on her face. She was barely audible over the low hum of the engine, but a tune cracked out of her dry throat as she flopped against the car. He looked at his horrified wife.

"Is she singing Happy Birthday?"

—

Rob Marshall took a break from poring over the police report about the two mysterious girls when he heard the giggles behind him.

"Any word on why the boss is tagging along this time?"

"I heard he's keeping an eye on Marshall."

Rob's ears caught the whispered mention of his name over the hum of the jet and removed one of his earbuds. He pretended to look at the clouds through the little window and listened in on Agents Brown and Lane.

"That doesn't surprise me after what happened last time."

Rob shook his head and the seat belt light turned off. He unbuckled himself and turned around in his seat to face the gossiping women.

"You two are worse than a sewing circle."

Lane held her hand over her heart and gave him a look of comical shock.

"Well, I never," she said.

Agent Brown stood up and pulled her dark hair back in a ponytail.

"You can't blame us, Rob. The winds of change are blowing, you know." Her eyes darted over to the seats at the front of the plane.

"What? Gorman's leaving? Is he transferring or getting promoted?"

Brown shrugged her shoulders and leaned over to put her hand on Rob's shoulder.

"Welcome to the sewing circle, Agent Marshall."

Rob laughed, but inside he imagined himself as the new Unit Chief at the Child Abduction Rapid Deployment office.

He always wanted to move up the ranks and the opportunity was staring him in the face now. The plane rumbled as it cut through the sky and Rob sat back down to put the distraction out of his head while he read over the police reports in the file. His fingers skimmed over the handwritten notes, medical assessments, and preliminary theories that the Los Angeles field office had forwarded to them. Gorman made a big deal of clearing his throat before he called everyone over.

Rob gathered his documents and followed Brown and Lane to join the others. The seats at the tiny meeting area at the front of the plane filled up fast as everyone gathered around to go over the case file together. Gorman straightened his stack of papers against the table as he looked around.

"Okay," he said, "you've all looked over the file?" The whole team nodded and Gorman was about to go on when Rob interjected.

"I don't get it, Chief," he said. "These girls aren't missing. Why does LA need our help?"

Gorman placed his hands down on his papers and sighed in exasperation. He gave a stern look to Rob before he continued.

"If I may?" Rob nodded at him having been put in his place. "The girls have yet to be identified and won't speak to anyone, but they seem to be deeply attached to one another. The doctors can only guess, but they put them anywhere from ages twelve to fourteen. They've likely been missing for years. Scour old reports, look at cold cases, dig deep. We're going to have to do what we can to get through to these girls and get them back to their families." Gorman paused and took a deep breath. "What's not in your file is that two young girls were abducted from their homes late last night. We are flying in to support the LA office and the Behavioral Analysis Unit because they believe that both of these cases are connected. They believe the same suspect set the first two girls free and took two new ones all in the same day. Based on what we know, these girls will be held for years. Or worse..."

Rob tried to connect the dots in his head and Agent Brown asked the same question he had on his mind.

"But Los Angeles is huge," she said. "How are we sure these aren't two random, unrelated kidnappings?"

Gorman nodded as if he had expected her to say those exact words.

"We aren't completely certain about the teenagers yet, but the missing girls both turned eight years old today."

- 2 -

Gorman looked around the table and his eyes stopped on each member of the team. Rob had seen that look before and knew it meant business. Gorman kept his gaze fixed on Rob and spoke.

"I want things done by the book," he said. "There's going to be a lot of attention on this case. From the media and the Bureau." The others nodded and Rob felt he was being directly addressed. "That means full co-operation and no pissing contests over jurisdiction. Understood?" The team's silence was enough for him and he went on. "Brown, you come with me to get set up at the police station. Lane and Benevides, I want you to get started with interviewing the witnesses. Marshall, I want you to meet Kyle Bishop at the hospital and get any information you can about the teen girls."

Rob tilted his head when he heard his assignment.

"Bishop? The BAU guy?"

"That's right."

"What about the girls? I thought they weren't talking."

Gorman took a long breath in through his nose.

"Maybe you could ask them a bunch of questions you already know the answer to." He knew Gorman wanted him on the sidelines because of the spotlight on the case, but Rob was more effective out in the field, chasing down leads.

Rob turned his hands up in defeat and didn't press the issue any further.

"Got it," he said.

"Just make sure you keep us apprised of your progress."

The group dispersed back to their seats and Benevides followed Rob.

"Hey, Marshall," he said as he sat down. "You gotta chill, man. Chief's got you on his radar. If you want that spot, you better fly straight. Know what I mean?"

"Who says I want his job?"

"Come on, bro. You ain't hard to read. You think you can do it better. Maybe you can, maybe not. But you won't even get a chance if you keep pressing his buttons."

"We'll see, Marcus."

"Anyway, enough politics. What do you make of this whole mess?"

Rob shook his head in thought.

"I don't know. It's a lot of moving parts, you know?"

Benevides nodded and they both studied the case files for the rest of the flight.

The pilot announced their arrival and the plane hit the runway with a slight jostle before it slowed to a stop. Everyone gathered their things and stepped out into the California sun. Two black SUVs awaited them and they split up. Benevides and Lane dropped Rob off at the hospital. He stood at the entrance and looked up at the building. The main structure was old and made of stone. Additions of glass and steel that had been built over the years shone in the sun. People shuffled to and fro as the first round of morning appointments were set to begin. The automatic sliding doors that graced the entrance hardly had a chance to close as patients and employees filed in and out.

Rob's phone buzzed against his thigh as he started to make his way up the steps. He pulled it out of his pocket just enough to peek at the screen. It was his wife, Gina. Rob slid the phone back in and let it vibrate away. If it was really important, she'd call back. Even if it wasn't, she'd still call back. He almost never answered her calls when he was away on a case anymore. It was the same conversation every time anyway. Everything was fine and there was nothing to worry about. He didn't have time to constantly placate her. Especially not today.

Rob followed the signs on the walls to the section of the hospital where the girls were being observed. He rode up a few floors on the elevator and knew he had the right floor when he saw the two police officers standing guard outside the rooms. They straightened up in anticipation as Rob approached. He pulled his identification from his shirt pocket and the older officer squinted as he read it over. Just as the officer nodded in satisfaction, the wide door opened and Agent Bishop stepped out. He closed the door with quiet and gentle care before he greeted Rob.

"Agent Marshall, thanks for coming." Bishop placed his hand on Rob's back and started to walk away from the door. Rob matched his slow pace and they stopped a few doors down to speak privately.

"Anything new, Kyle?"

"Actually, yes," Bishop glanced down at his tie. It was loosened and he adjusted it back in place. "When the doctors tried to put them in separate rooms, they lashed out. They didn't want to be apart and called out to each other by first name." He pointed to the file under Rob's arm to get him to open it. Bishop pointed at each photograph as he labeled them. "Jessie and Sarah."

"Anything else?"

"Not really," Bishop said as he adjusted his tie one last time. "These girls have a strong bond with each other, but otherwise won't speak a word to anyone. It will take some time to get through to them."

Rob didn't have the psychology background that everyone in the BAU seemed to have and he knew that he didn't have the skills needed to be effective inside that room.

"What can I do to help?"

"Check in with the teams, have them look at missing persons cases with those names." Rob closed his case file and Bishop looked him dead in the eyes. "These young ladies are the key to finding the missing girls, Rob."

He left Rob and muttered with the police officers before he went back in as gently as he emerged. Rob checked his phone and the signal was low so he wandered the hall, phone held up like a divining rod, in search of better reception. Near a window, it gained a strong connection and he dialed Chief Gorman and relayed the information he'd obtained.

"Got it, Marshall. We'll check it out." Gorman hung up unceremoniously and Rob stood in the long hallway as nurses and doctors whizzed past with more purpose than he had at the moment. He tapped his feet, paced around, and stayed in the same general area awaiting a call back.

Finally, his phone rang. It was Gina again. He sent it straight to voicemail and resumed his ritualistic puttering. Ten painfully uneventful minutes had gone by when Agent Brown called with the results of their search.

"Nothing matching those names in state records. We're expanding the search, though."

Rob sighed at the lack of news.

"Right. Keep me posted," he said and hung up, forgoing any pleasantries. He paced the length of the hall and as he passed by the room that Bishop and the girls were in, he could have sworn he heard them singing Happy Birthday. The two officers on guard eyeballed each other as they listened in as well. Before Rob could try and make sense of it, he received a message on his phone from Bishop. This time, he rushed to where he knew he could get a signal and called Agent Brown.

"Dana, run a national search. Female missing persons, of any age, whose birthday is today."

- 3 -

The man heard a stirring sound in the corner of the dark room. Between the muted thumps of the sewing machine and his own heavy, concentrated breath, a tiny body shuffled in the bed behind him. He raised his head up as a deer would at the unexpected snap of a trod upon a stick. A little groan, an adjustment for comfort, and at last the sounds of resumed slumber. The man went back to his work and smiled with satisfaction that the sedative hadn't worn off yet. He wasn't ready.

Once his work was done, he held the navy blue garment up in front of himself. The bold white collar was just like the picture this time and even the lace trim on the bottom, which he had struggled with before, was perfect. Everything was just as it should be. He looked over his shoulder to once again judge his sizing estimations. Without accurate measurements, he was uncertain how well it would fit, but it looked about right.

He set it down with the other one and picked up the shears he'd used to trim the fabric earlier. His mother had always told him that they were never to be used for anything else. Not for paper. Not for arts and crafts. These were special scissors. The man grunted at the memory and smacked his temple in quick succession with the base of his palm. He shook the thought away and hovered over one of the beds. There was one more thing to do before he could begin.

He ran his hand through the sleeping girl's long brown hair and held it out against the light. It was just the right color, but still too long. He tensed the strands and snipped off a section. Not too short. It would take far too long to grow back if he cut it too short. It was best to go slow and be sure. The man started slowly, timid and unsure, until he moved with the confidence of a Hollywood stylist. She stayed asleep while he worked, which pleased him. When he finished, he gently brushed aside the excess clippings and pressed her bangs down with his hand. They would take a little time to settle into the right position, but he was satisfied.

The man swiveled around on his knees to face the adjacent bed. Her hair was lighter, but still acceptable. His fingers straightened her hair out and she stirred again with a groan. He pulled his hand back and watched her eyelids flutter against the soft yellow light of the bulb overhead. He didn't have much time left before she would wake so he went about trimming her hair to the proper length. Even rushed, he matched the style of the old photograph on the nightstand that separated the two beds.

No sooner had the man finished than the girl opened her eyes. Drowsy contentment gave way to confusion as she took in her surroundings. The slow transition from sleep to wakeful awareness fascinated the man and he greeted her with a smile. The girl recoiled in fear, realizing she was not in her own bed. Her eyes now dashed around in search of familiarity where none would be found. She backed herself up against the corner of the cement wall and the thin metal bed frame. The man had put his hands up to show he meant no harm but had forgotten about the scissors clutched in his grasp. He quickly set them down to alleviate her fear. Not the nicest thing to wake up to, he supposed. The girl spotted the snipped hair about her and felt her head. Confusion mounted in her eyes and she looked past the man to the opposite bed. Some errant clumps of hair remained strewn around her, too. Tears welled in her already bloodshot eyes and the man watched her face tighten and twist itself up for a cry.

"Shh..." The man pressed a finger to his lips and glanced back over his shoulder at the sleeping girl. "Don't cry, Sarah."

She sniffled back the impending tears. "My name is Kayla."

"Shh!" He implored her again.

"I want my mommy," she whispered as a tear skipped down her cheek. The man snatched up the shears from the floor and pointed them at her. His voice was low, but full of authority.

"Behave yourself, Sarah."

The commotion caused the other girl to stir but not awaken. He stood and gathered a broom and dustpan to clean up the remaining hair. As he shook the pan against a small metal trash can, the sleeping girl sat up, equally alarmed as the first.

"Good morning, Jessie," the man said. "I hope you slept well."

The two girls exchanged glances and he held up the dresses he'd made, one in each hand. He smiled proudly and laid them down on the foot of each mattress.

"Get dressed, girls we've got a big day today."

"Who are you? Where's my mommy? Where's my daddy?"

"Don't worry about that, Jessie. I'll take care of you now."

"I'm not Jessie."

Sarah shook her head at the girl to get her to stop. The man stayed calm this time.

"That's enough of that, Jessie."

"Please, mister," Sarah said. "I want to go home now."

He kicked the metal bed frame and it clanged out an echo in the concrete room. He had startled them, but regained his composure. He had forgotten how difficult they could be in the beginning. Though his patience was tested, he had important things to do and only a few hours to do them all.

"No more talking back, girls. Big Brother is going to make sure you have a great day."

"Who's Big Brother?"

"Me, silly," the man said as he knelt down at the small fridge in the corner of the room. "Now, I normally wouldn't say this is the best breakfast, but today is a special day, isn't it?" He turned around to show them the cake he had prepared the night before. He set the candles alight and sang to them as he gingerly approached them. The flames flickered with each careful step. He set it down on the nightstand between them and finished his song.

"Happy birthday to you."

- 4 -

After another agonizing wait, Agent Brown called back with the results of the search.

"Rob, I've got some possibilities, but the names don't match. I sent everything to your phone."

"The signal here is unreliable. I'll call you back when I look it over."

Rob headed to the elevator when Agent Bishop stuck his head out from the room and waved him down.

"Rob, what's the word from HQ?"

"A few matches, but with different names. I was just about to go—"

"Not yet," Bishop interrupted. "Come inside with me first. You should hear this."

He led Rob into the darkened room. Whether from not knowing what to expect or a feeling of being out of his element, Rob tiptoed with trepidation as he entered. The curtains were closed to block out the sun and the overhead lights all turned off. The fluorescent glow of the hall came through the small window in the door. As his eyes adjusted he saw two empty beds to his left. The sliding trays that were normally used for eating meals in bed were pushed into the corner and huddled together underneath were the two girls. They were still dressed as they were found, disheveled and dirty. One girl rocked the other in her arms and mumbled something with each sway. Rob was taken aback and let a gasp slip out. No matter how many horrible things he'd come across in this job, he never got used to it. Bishop held his hands out to the girls to reassure them and spoke softly.

"It's okay. It's okay. This is my friend, Rob. He's one of the good guys."

Rob didn't know exactly how to react so he flashed a nervous smile and gave them a friendly wave. He leaned over to Bishop and asked for instruction.

"So what do I..."

"Just listen." He pointed to the corner as the girls resumed their embrace. They rocked back and forth. The hum of ventilation and people passing in the hall drowned out their words, but Rob eventually tuned it all out and focused on their voices.

"He doesn't love us anymore."
"Yes, he does. He's our Big Brother."
"Will Big Brother take care of us?"
"Big Brother will keep us safe."
"He doesn't love us anymore."
"Yes, he does. He's our Big Brother."
They continued on, as if stuck in an endless loop and Bishop led Rob back out to the hallway. Rob squinted against the bright light as his eyes readjusted.

"Okay, who's Big Brother?"
"I doubt he's an actual sibling of either of them, but don't dismiss the possibility."
"How long do you think he had them?"
"They're exhibiting signs of years of conditioning," Bishop said. "Go over the matches you got and let me know if there's anything I can use to get them talking."
"Got it."
Rob pressed for the elevator and went downstairs. The temperature had risen as the morning went on. He shielded his phone from the light and read over what Brown had sent. He called her up to get some more details.

"Hey Rob, I was just trying to call you.

We ran the aging software on all the pictures from the missing persons files. They match Erika James and Abbie Friesen. They were taken from their homes five years ago on their birthday. Benevides and Lane are splitting up to go get their parents."

"I need you to check something for me," Rob said.

"What are we looking for?"

"Did either of them have a brother?"

"Let's see. Yes. Darren Friesen was nineteen when Abbie disappeared. Erika is an only child."

"Where is he now?" The clicks of the keyboard were audible through the phone as Brown searched.

"Attended San Diego State, dropped out after two years, a few construction jobs here and there, and then... moved back to LA. Last known address is an apartment in Burbank."

"In Illinois?"

"There's more than one Burbank, Chicago boy. It's about a half hour north of you. I'll come pick you up."

"No need. I just want to show him some pictures, ask some questions. What's the address?"

"I'll send it to you."

"Thanks." Rob hung up and realized that he didn't have a vehicle. He looked around the parking lot and spotted a black SUV with a government tag on the back. It had to be Bishop's. Rob went back up to the room and waved Bishop out to the hall.

"What is it?"

"We got their real names. I sent you a file with everything we found."

Bishop seemed pleased as he looked it over.

"Good work, Rob."

"Thanks. Was that your truck I saw outside?"

"Yes," Bishop said with an air of suspicion.

"Mind if I borrow it? My team just kind of dropped me off here."

Bishop fished in his pocket and produced a set of keys without hesitation. He unhooked a large key from the rest and held it up in front of himself.

"Just be careful with it."

Rob smiled at him and grabbed the key.

"Man, you roll a truck over one time and never hear the end of it." Rob scanned Bishop's face for a reaction, but he remained as stone-faced as always. "I won't be long," Rob said. "Just have to check something out."

Bishop returned to the room, armed with his wealth of new information, without another word.

Rob programmed the address into the GPS and headed out. As he drove, he thought about Chief Gorman. He wanted to show that stuffed suit that he could get things done. If he could crack the case, he'd be a frontrunner for the promotion too.

The voice on the GPS informed him that he was about to arrive. He turned into a parking lot in desperate need of repair. The pink and white apartment building looked like it used to be one of those two story motels. No balconies or patios. Just a cement walkway lined by a lime green railing to give it a real tropical look. As he climbed the stairs, a pool that hadn't seen much but rain water came into view. Dead palm leaves lay in the bottom amid of puddle of brown water. The unmistakable sounds of daytime talk shows blared out as he passed by the windows. A few curious faces peeked from behind curtains and quickly retreated when the sunlight reflected off of his badge. Rob reached the unit he was after and double checked his file. The nail that once held the metal number two upright had disappeared and left the digit dangling upside down on the door. Rob thumped his fist against the door and called out.

"Darren Friesen."

A young man's voice hollered back from inside.

"Who is it?"

"I'm with the FBI," Rob called back. "I want to ask you some questions."

There was no response this time. Rob heard a scrambling commotion as he leaned his ear toward the door. He pounded on the door again.

"Open up, Darren!"

Rob heard a scream that sounded further away than the initial response. He threw his head back and cracked his neck, readying himself to enter by force. He took a stride back on the walkway and launched his foot toward the door handle. He planted it right beside the imitation brass knob and the cheap door cracked as it swung open and slammed against the wall.

He hurled himself into the room, weapon drawn and pointed skyward. He quickly scanned his surroundings. The dirty couch, rickety lawn chair, and small coffee table littered with beer bottles and drug paraphernalia seemed almost expected. He covered the distance to the small bedroom with three quick steps and found it in equal disarray but empty. The messy little kitchen had a pile of old crusted dishes in the sink but was also empty. He peeked his head around the corner of the bathroom, ready to confront and subdue. The window was open and the screen had been bent upward and outward.

"Son of a bitch," he muttered and holstered his gun. He bolted out the front door and rushed back down the stairs. He sprinted around the pool enclosure and behind the building. The burnt grass crinkled under his feet and he spotted a scruffy young man running away with a slight limp. He turned a corner, but Rob could still see his bright blue baseball cap bobbing up and down over a wooden fence. He ran faster and swung himself around the bend. Down an alley lined with fences and littered with metal trash cans that had been kicked over, he spotted the bright blue hat on the ground, well behind the head that had once carried it. He chased after Darren and came out of the alley onto a busy street. He searched around, unsure of which way Darren had fled. The sharp skidding of tires drew his attention left and he saw Darren hop over the hood of the car as it screeched to a halt.

"Freeze!" Rob yelled out as he charged toward him. Darren gave a startled look around and rushed down another alleyway between two buildings. Rob rushed toward him and gained some ground as he weaved through the stopped cars and bystanders who scurried around at the sight of his gun. He hurried into the alleyway and heard the distant wail of police sirens, unsure if they were dispatched to help him or just a matter of happenstance. Darren turned another corner ahead of him, not nearly as far ahead anymore. Rob heard some incomprehensible shouting from people on the fire escapes high above and pushed himself to go even faster. The scream of the sirens grew louder as they approached. He wheeled around the corner and a flash of light preceded a loud crackle like the clap of nearby thunder. He was forced backward and hurtled to the ground in a tumbling heap. The last thing he remembered was a searing hot pain before his head hit the unforgiving pavement and darkness whisked him away.

- 5 -

Rob was surrounded by a crowd of faceless people. Where their eyes should have been, were only black pits. Their mouths, equally black, spewed forth flashes of light like he saw in the alley. The blank faces hovered over his body and chanted.

"Marshall, Marshall, Marshall..."

The hypnotic chorus coincided with the blasts of white light as the crowd huddled in closer and closer to him. One of the faceless beings reached its hand toward him as the horrible taunting reached a fever pitch. Its long, claw-like finger pressed against his shoulder, so hot that it pierced him and sunk into his flesh. They continued to shout his name and Rob squirmed against the pain, but he could only manage to shake his head in protest and terror.

"Marshall! Marshall!"

Rob quickly propped himself up on his elbows and the crowd of faces washed away in a harsh light, brighter than the flashes they sparked out at him.

"Marshall!"

Rob looked around for the soft voice as his eyes adjusted to the waking world.

"It's me."

"Dana?"

He lifted his arm to rub his eyes, but a searing pain shot down his left arm.

"Easy, Rob. You're in the hospital." Dana said. "You got popped in the shoulder and damn near cracked your skull, too."

"What?" Rob shook his head and the details started to fill in as he became more alert. "Darren?"

"LAPD picked him up down the street right after it happened."

"I can't believe that little prick shot me."

Dana slumped back in her chair with a sigh.

"That was pretty stupid of you, Marshall."

"I was just going to ask him some questions."

"Without backup," Dana reminded him.

"How was I supposed to know he would run? Or shoot at me?"

"That's just it, Rob. You never know."

Rob exhaled as he thought about all the possible ways this incident could be held against him. This wasn't just a wrecked vehicle that the team could joke about later on. He had to make sure it wasn't for nothing. He groaned and hoisted himself up in the bed. Dana stood up and held her hands out block him.

"What do you think you're doing?"

"I'm gonna go question Darren."

"Like hell," Dana said. "You need to stay here and get checked out."

"I'm fine. Just a flesh wound." Rob swung his legs over the side of the bed and noticed his bare legs sticking out from under a green hospital gown. He looked behind him and Dana held up a plastic bag with a look of resigned disapproval as she shook her head at him. She tossed the bag on the bed and headed to the door.

"Hurry up," she said. "I'll give you a ride."

Rob remembered then Bishop's SUV was still at Darren's apartment building. He got dressed and met Dana out in the hall. A nurse rushed over from her desk and gave him a stern recommendation to stay, but Rob refused, so she made him sign a mountain of paperwork before he could leave. She gave him a sling to wear so the wound wouldn't tear and an endless list of instructions to follow that he just nodded along to.

They walked down the long hallway and Rob felt a familiarity in his surroundings.

"I think we should check in with Bishop," he said as he pulled out his phone. There was no signal.

"Trust me, Rob," Dana said, "he knows." She pointed to the logo on the glass door that led outside. It was the same hospital and Bishop was just upstairs.

As Dana drove along with the slow traffic, Rob rubbed the back of his head. There was a new bump there and he winced from the pressure.

"So have you talked to Gorman?" Rob asked. Dana kept her eyes forward and nodded. Rob's phone rang and he looked at the display. Gina again. "You didn't tell my wife what happened, did you?" Dana shook her head in the negative and Rob ignored the call yet again.

"You're not gonna talk to her?"

"She'll just get all worked up," Rob said. "It can wait until we get back. What did Gorman say?"

"Nothing good." Dana didn't take her eyes off the road, even though they were at a dead stop.

"I was just trying to—"

"I know what you were trying to do, Rob," Dana snapped at him. She continued with a quiet but angry tone. "You think if you go out and prove you're some kind of hot shot it'll get you that promotion. Well, it won't."

Rob had never seen Dana like that. Her usual calm manner was missing through the scolding.

"Whatever," Rob said, "I was just trying to help solve this thing."

"You can't help anyone if you're dead." Dana turned her eyes back to the road and they rode the rest of the way in silence. The police station was mobbed by reporters waiting for their next scoop. Gorman wasn't kidding about the media presence. Rob had never seen such a frenzy. Dana pushed through ahead of him and he followed close behind her as he ignored the microphones thrust at him. Two officers opened the doors for them as they entered the station. The noise inside was just as frenetic. Detectives, feds, and uniformed cops scurried about. Gorman popped his head out from behind a tinted glass door across the room.

"Marshall! Get in here!"

Rob turned to Dana said, "Time to face the music."

He marched toward the office, careful not to wince from the pain in his shoulder as Gorman stared him down. Rob approached with his hand held up in front of him.

"I can explain, sir," he said, but Gorman cut him off.

"I don't want to hear it, Marshall. I don't have time for excuses and I don't have time to waste reprimanding you right now. We'll deal with this when we get back to Washington."

"Fair enough," Rob said. He was relieved to escape a scolding, albeit temporarily.

"Your suspect is in room 3. You better make something out of this, understood?"

Rob nodded and left before Gorman changed his mind about chewing him out. He jerked his head to get Dana to come with him and she hurried up alongside him. They entered the observation room on the other side of the two-way mirror. An officer sat in a metal chair with his feet propped up on the ledge of the mirror while he picked at his fingernails. He tried to bumble out an excuse as he scurried to his feet.

"Agents, I was just about to—"

"Don't worry about it," Rob said as he peered through the mirror. "Is he saying anything?"

"No sir, not really."

"We'll take it from here." Rob held the door open and the officer left. Dana and Rob stared through the glass and studied Darren. One minute he scratched at his arms and neck with an anxious look on his face and the next he had a look of depressed resignation as he ran his palms over the metal table. The shackles clanged against the edge and Darren slapped his hands down in anger.

"Someone get me some damn water!"

He looked right at the mirror and Rob went out to the hallway. He looked back and forth and spotted a water cooler. He filled two paper cups and headed back. The officer posted at the door let him into the interrogation room and locked the door behind him.

"Finally," Darren said as he came in. He must not have recognized Rob at first as he wiggled his outstretched fingers for the drink. "Andy Griffith out there said I just missed the lunch run and he hasn't been back since. What kind of shit is that?"

Rob didn't answer him and set each cup down at the very edge of the table, as far away from Darren's reaching grasp as possible. He eased into the chair opposite and leaned back, one leg propped up on his knee.

He reached over to the edge of the table and plucked one of the paper cups. Without breaking eye contact, he stared Darren down as he gulped down the water. After an exaggerated exhale of refreshment, he sat up straight and leaned on his elbows. It hurt his shoulder, but he tried to ignore it.

"So," Rob said, "you ready to talk now?"

Darren finally had a spark of recognition in his eyes as he glanced between Rob's face and shoulder. He slumped down in his seat as he realized who Rob was.

"Listen, man—"

Rob held up a finger to interrupt him. He pulled out his notepad and flipped a few sheets over. He looked at the blank page and shook his head back and forth.

"Tsk, tsk, Darren." Rob ran his finger down the empty lines and rhymed off what he remembered from earlier.

"Possession, intent to distribute, obstruction, carrying a concealed weapon, public endangerment, attempted murder of a federal agent..." Rob looked up to gauge Darren's reaction. He had resumed his frantic scratching and left red marks on his neck. "Well, it just keeps going and going." Rob closed the notepad and placed it on the table. Darren's eyes were wide with panic.

"N-n-n-no, man. It's not like that. I mean, I... I didn't know you were a fed. I figured you were some gangster, trying to take me out."

"Why would a gangster try to take you out?"

Darren shook his head like he had said too much and didn't respond.

"You get a lot of gangsters coming around claiming to be from the FBI?"

"Well, no."

Rob breathed in through his nose in frustration and took a different approach.

"I'm gonna level with you, Darren. It doesn't look good for you." Darren's fingers crept back up to his neck as he listened. "But, I'm a forgiving kind of guy. I can forgive the drugs. I can forgive you for running away. I can even forgive you for this." Rob pointed to his shoulder and Darren exhaled in relief. "All I want to know is where the girls are."

"Girls?" Darren said as if he hadn't heard him. "What girls?"

"What happened? The first two escaped so you grabbed two more?"

"What the hell are you talking about, man?"

"Or maybe they just got too old for your liking. Yeah, you look like you have a preference."

"You're nuts, dude," Darren said as he slumped back in his chair. His eyes drifted to the cup of water on the edge of the table. Rob recaptured his attention as he stood and slapped his hand down on the table.

"Don't play stupid! We found your sister and her friend. Now I want to know where the other girls are!"

Darren held his hands up as high as the shackles would allow as he stared up at Rob.

"My sister?"

"And it won't be long before she starts talking. So just do the right thing and tell me where Emily and Kayla are."

Darren's eyes fluttered around and his mouth gaped open. Rob realized then that he didn't have the right guy.

"Abbie's alive..." Darren said again as he stared at the table. Rob hung his head, frustrated. He slid the cup of water in front of Darren, but he ignored it, locked in a distant stare at the revelation. Rob could tell he had no idea about Abbie or any of the other girls. There was a knock on the door and Dana stuck her head in as she waved Rob over to her. He kept his eyes on Darren as Dana whispered in his ear.

"It's not him, Rob."

"I know."

They left Darren alone in the room and spoke in the hallway.

"Fuck," Rob said. "Gorman's gonna crucify me for this."

Dana cocked her head to draw Rob's attention down the hallway.

"Incoming."

Gorman stomped over with his arms out in disbelief. Rob shrugged as he approached.

"It wasn't him, Chief. At least we can still get him for all the other charges."

Without taking his eyes off of Rob, Gorman knocked on the door to the adjacent room and the officer hurried out.

"Cut him loose," he said. "Take him to the hospital so he can see his sister."

The officer looked confused.

"Really?"

Rob interjected himself into the conversation.

"Chief, this kid shot me. In public. You're just gonna let him go?"

Gorman didn't address Rob but spoke to the officer.

"Forget it all. Drop the charges."

Rob walked down the hall in a huff and got himself another paper cup of water. A few minutes later, the officer escorted Darren away. Rob and Dana followed a few steps behind them. Gorman watched them as they walked off; hands on hips, head shaking in disapproval. Rob could practically feel Gorman's sharp breath as it shot out from his nostrils. The officer stopped at the front desk and signed a bunch of papers while they returned Darren's things to him.

Rob stood at the desk as he watched Darren stutter-step away in confusion. He hadn't gotten any closer to finding the missing girls and got shot in the process. Wasted time, wasted resources, and nothing to show for it but a bullet wound.

"Back to the drawing board," Rob said. Dana smacked him on his good shoulder.

"Come on, Rob. Let's go pick up Bishop's truck and head over to the hospital."

- 6 -

The man collected the paper plates and plastic cutlery from Jessie and Sarah as he hummed a tune. After he tidied up, he handed them each a small box, wrapped in pink paper with a white bow on top.

"What kind of birthday party would be complete without gifts?"

The girls looked at each other and they opened them slowly. Jessie had tears in her eyes and the man touched her leg to soothe her.

"Do you not like it, Jessie? I got you both the same doll so there'd be no fighting. Twins like to have the same things anyway, don't they?"

Jessie looked up at him with streaks of tears on her cheeks.

"We're not twins," she said and looked at Sarah. "I want my mommy." The man snatched the white-faced doll from her hand and shook it in front of her face.

"Stop that!"

He rushed over to his desk drawer and held a syringe up to the light. He flicked it with his finger while he watched the liquid drip out from the tip of the needle. Sarah looked at him with frightened eyes.

"Please don't," she said.

"Quiet!" He stepped toward Jessie and she cowered in the corner of her small bed.

"I'm sorry, I'm sorry," she said. The man sunk the needle in the flesh of her arm. She let out a short yelp and he lowered the plunger halfway. He slowly pulled the needle out and within minutes, the drug had worked its way through her system. The man rested her head in the crook of his arm and laid her down on her pillow. Jessie looked up at him and managed a soft whisper.

"I'm sorry."

He stroked her hair and smiled at her. Sarah sniffled behind him and he turned to face her, needle in hand. Sarah shook her head in protest as he leaned down toward her. He held Sarah down and gave her the remaining doses. She clutched her new doll in her arms as he felt her resistance fade. He stood up and loomed over the docile girls.

"I'm your Big Brother," the man said. "I will take care of you. I will keep you safe."

The man gathered his calm and went upstairs to pore over old photo albums and scrapbooks. He absorbed every detail as he flipped through the pages. The flashes of memories, though faded by the years, brought him back to that day long ago.

The smell of fresh meat on the grill filled the boy's nose. His mother had been to the butcher the day before. The sounds of laughter filled the open backyard. Aunts and uncles and cousins all gathered. His father flipped the meat and it sizzled against the hot metal. His business partners from the law firm stood around him, drinks in hand, as they chattered about the various techniques for the perfect steak. The twins frolicked hand in hand in their navy blue dresses with white polka dots. They swung their dolls as they skipped across the grass, singing a song about sisterhood.

After the delicious lunch, the children all sped off to play. Some played tag, others raced around aimlessly. The boy meandered about until he found himself behind the tool shed, digging in a dirt patch for possible buried treasure. His mother had gone inside to prepare the cake. The boy heard the squeak of the screen door and knew it was time to light the candles and sing Happy Birthday. The raucous laughter died down and shouting ensued. The boy peeked around the corner of the shed and saw all his family members looking away from the cake and out at the open expanse of the backyard. His father stormed out toward a stranger who approached from the field. He yelled and pointed his finger. He looked angry and waved his hand at the mysterious stranger like he was a stray dog who had wandered into the wrong yard. Dressed all in black from head to toe, the stranger kept his course despite the warning. His father stopped as the stranger came closer. The rest of the gathering had taken notice and pointed their outstretched arms toward the man. They looked as confused as the boy was as to who this man could be and why his father wanted him to go away.

The boy looked back at the stranger and his father. The sun gleamed off the metal barrel of the shotgun as the man swung it from behind his back. Only yards apart now, the stranger screamed.

"You ruined my life!"

His father held his hands up in protest and a loud blast exploded from the end of the weapon that sent him hurtling back and down to the ground. Screams filled the air interspersed by more thunderous booms. Bodies scurried and scattered, falling to the ground as they were cut down by the spray of pellets. The boy spotted the twins, hands still clutched together as they ran toward the house. The stranger whirled around and pumped the handgrip of his gun. He trained his aim on the girls from behind them and, with a single blast, they tumbled to the ground. The boy curled back behind the shed to hide. He listened in terror as more shots rang out. The screams grew fewer and fewer. The shots were quieter as if from a smaller gun, but they still made the boy gasp each time. He sat in the dirt with his back pressed against the tool shed. He pulled his knees up to his chest and ignored the tears as they dripped down, careful not to sniffle. He stayed as silent as he could and barely took a breath.

The shots ceased as did the screams and the boy mustered the courage to look again. He poked his around the shed slowly and just enough to see the stranger. The shotgun lay at his feet and he held a pistol. He seemed to survey the carnage around him as he slowly turned his head from side to side. Sirens in the distance made him cock his head. The nearest neighbor was a far walk away, but they could have heard the shots. As the sound of the sirens drew closer, the stranger held the pistol to his temple. The muted discharge was accompanied by a fountainous burst of red against the light blue sky. The stranger crumpled to the ground in a bloody heap. The boy crawled out further from his hiding place toward his sisters. His tears left wet marks in the dirt as he trudged along, unable to find the nerve to stand.

When he reached the twins, he couldn't even tell which one was which. One laid face down and an expanding pool of blood flowed out from her back. The other coughed and little red bubbles lined her lips as she stared up at the sky. The white polka dots on her dress were stained pink. She pawed at the boy's hand and squeezed it tight. More blood streaked out from the corner of her lips as she opened her mouth to speak. She gasped and choked as she coughed out more little bubbles. Her tight grip loosened on his hand and went limp as she let out a final, wet exhale. The boy sat there, hand in hand with his sister, and watched the flames flicker on the candles atop the birthday cake. Each one dripped the white wax down onto the icing and, eventually, snuffed out one by one with a curly string of smoke. The sirens wailed louder as they reached the house. Policemen rushed by the picnic table and the last of the candles blew out in their wake.

- 7 -

Dana didn't speak to Rob as she drove him back to Darren's apartment building. Rob didn't mind, though. He ran through the case in his head. Maybe he overlooked some small detail that would let everything fall into place. For the whole ride, he stared out the window. Not at the sights of the City of Angels but just past it all, as if he could catch a glimpse behind the scenes of the universe.

Dana dropped him off at the SUV and he drove himself back. He hoped Bishop had made some headway with the girls at the hospital and went to check in with him. When Rob arrived, Darren was already there to see his sister. The two officers stationed outside the room stood shoulder to shoulder to block his entry to the room. Darren paced back and forth in front of them like he was planning his best option to break through the human blockade. His eyes were full of aggression and contempt for the two policemen. So sharp was his focus on the obstacle he faced, Rob had gotten close to him undetected. He leaned forward and whispered.

"Is there a problem, Darren?"

He jumped at the sound of Rob's voice and turned around to face him. Darren tilted his head back in disbelief when he realized it was Rob.

"Great, now you're here. These pigs won't let me see my sister."

Before Rob could say anything, Bishop came out of the room.

"What's going on here?"

Rob motioned down the hallway.

"Let's talk over here."

They walked away from the room and the officers as well. Bishop glanced between Rob and Darren, awaiting an explanation.

"Who's this?" he asked Rob.

"Darren Friesen," Rob said. "He's Abbie's brother."

"I wanna see her," Darren said. At the other end of the hall, the elevator door opened and Benevides held his arm against the bumper to let an old couple out. They looked tired and defeated by the years. The woman walked with her arms tight to her midsection, tissue in hand to dab at her raw red eyes. Benevides beckoned Rob to join him. Darren squinted down the hallway at the old couple.

"Mom? Dad?" He stutter-stepped toward them in the same confused manner with which he left the police station.

"Darren," the mother said with arms outstretched to him. The man glared at Darren as he approached and spoke with suspicion in his voice.

"What are you doing here?"

Darren looked unaffected and hugged his mother. He pointed at Rob as they separated.

"This FBI guy told me about Abbie." Rob couldn't help but chuckle at the massive omission of details. "I came to see her." They walked toward the room.

Bishop made sure to intercept the family reunion before it ever began. The officers stood behind him like a wall.

"I'm afraid we can't go in just yet," Bishop said. "She's not ready."

"What are you talking about, dude? I wanna see my sister."

"Please, follow me," Bishop said, "I need to ask you some questions first." He took them to an empty room and closed the door behind him. Benevides pointed his chin at Rob's shoulder.

"How're you feeling?"

"I've been better."

Benevides nodded his head in approval and moved on from the small talk.

"Lane's bringing the other girl's parents. Should be here any minute. Dana is downstairs waiting for you. I'll stay here with Bishop."

"Sounds good."

Rob took the elevator down and figured Dana had been assigned to be his shadow and keep him out of trouble. When he got outside, Dana was on her phone and held her finger up to Rob.

"Yep," she said as she nodded. "Yep. Okay. Got it."

"What is it?"

"I'll tell you on the way. Let's go."

"I'll drive," Rob said.

"No need, lead foot. We're going back inside."

"Why?"

"The BAU worked up a profile. They narrowed it down to a few names and one of them works here."

Rob hurried alongside Dana. They held their badges up as they rushed through the halls and asked directions along the way. Dana briefed Rob on the team's findings as they went. The hospital administrator's office was tucked away in the recesses of the hospital. Eventually, they were led by a helpful security guard who gave them access to the restricted areas. He showed them to the receptionist and went on his way.

Rob found that security guards were always happy to help the real authorities. They could go home, tell a story about assisting an FBI investigation and feel big about themselves. Cops, on the other hand, were resistant and territorial. From the chief all the way down to the uniforms, they didn't like their toes stepped on. Rob liked the eager security guards better. Dana flashed her badge at the receptionist and she showed them in. They sat in the barely cushioned chairs that must have been overstock from the waiting rooms around the institution. Across the desk was an empty seat that looked decidedly more comfortable and cushy, meant for longer stretches of use. The light sparkled off of the gold framing of the nameplate on the desk. A single picture frame stood on the neatly organized desk, tilted just enough that Rob could see the family of three in a posed photo that could have easily doubled as a Christmas card. Rob's phone buzzed in his pocket. It was Gina again. Since he had a moment, he was about to finally answer his wife's call, but a woman rushed into the office with a bundle of folders under her arm.

"Sorry to keep you waiting, agents," she said. "Even these days, some things still require signatures and paperwork."

Rob laughed as he remembered the pile of reports on his desk in Washington.

"We work for the government," he said. "We know a thing or two about paperwork."

"I suppose you would," she said as she set the folders down, squared exactly on the corner of her tidy desk. The woman smiled and held her hand out to them from across the desk.

"Betsy Carrigan. I assume you're here about those girls upstairs. How can I help?"

They all shook hands and Dana consulted her phone for some details.

"Our behavioral analysts believe that the perpetrator may have a medical background or work in the field. The girls upstairs, Abbie and Erika, were drugged repeatedly over a period of years with a powerful sedative."

Dana turned her phone to Betsy to show her the long, scientific name of the drug. Betsy nodded as she read it.

"That would be used to calm erratic behavior which could stop us from treating a patient. It's not needed often, but can be very effective."

Rob readied his notepad.

"Who would have access to something like that, Ms. Carrigan?"

"All the nurses and doctors. There are multiple storage rooms throughout the hospital, all with secure keypad locks."

Dana looked pleased.

"So they all have unique access codes that you cross-check against inventory?"

Betsy shook her head.

"Not in the budget I'm afraid. It's one code per locker."

"Too bad," Rob said. "Any inventory discrepancies?"

"Not to my knowledge."

Dana stood up to thank her and shake hands. Rob wanted to cover all the bases before they left though.

"When you have a moment," he said, "could you get us a list of nurses and doctors with access to those lockers?"

"It might take some time but, yes. I can do that." Betsy took Dana's business card and gestured to the door. "Let me walk you out. It's easy to get lost if you don't know the way."

Betsy walked ahead of them, still seemingly in a rush. Rob thought of how many people in all of the hospitals that would have easy access to the drug. He nudged Dana's arm with is elbow.

"Needle in a haystack."

She nodded in agreement.

"More like a needle in a pile of needles. Maybe we can get something from the employee files, though. We just need more to go with it."

Once they got to the main hallway, Betsy bade them farewell and turned on her heel to head back. In her haste, she slammed into a janitor and his cart, sending his load of spray bottles and brooms sprawling across the floor. Rob helped Betsy back to her feet as Dana and the janitor picked up the spilled items. The bumbling janitor had a look of shame as he watched Betsy compose herself after the fall.

"I'm sorry, ma'am," he said with his eyes aimed at the floor.

"It's quite all right," Betsy said and dismissed him. Rob gathered her folders from the floor and handed them back to her. "Thank you," she said as they all watched the janitor scurry away. He struggled with a keypad that beeped at him with every incorrect entry. Betsy walked over to help him get into the room and rejoined the agents.

"Sorry about that, agents. New hires take some time to adjust and I had to replace someone on short notice."

Rob kept his eyes on the door as he spoke.

"Is that one of the secure storage areas?"

"It is."

"So the maintenance staff have access, too?"

"Yes." Betsy sounded confused by his question. Dana had a look on her face that echoed Betsy's tone. Rob carried on without explanation.

"What happened to the previous janitor?"

Betsy sighed, not at Rob but as if she was recalling a taxing time.

"Strangest thing, Agent Marshall. Our old janitor, been here for years and years, just up and quit because he couldn't get a day off. He made a big scene of it, too. Yelling and carrying on." Betsy shook her head at the recollection. Dana still looked at Rob, unsure of where he was going with this line of questioning.

"What day did he want off?" Rob said.

"Today, actually. He wouldn't even say why. He just kept hollering about how important it was to him." Betsy shook her head at how crazy it sounded and, looking around her first, walked back towards the administrative area. Dana gave Rob a knowing glance and they spoke in unison. "That's our guy."

They hurried down the hall to catch up with Betsy Carrigan.

- 8 -

Rob and Dana gathered all the information they could about their new suspect. Betsy made phone calls, rushed around the offices of the hospital, and flipped through pages and computer files like a whirlwind. They emailed what they could and took the physical copies of everything else. Dana walked at a brisk pace as she tried to phone Chief Gorman.

"The reception is crap here," she said. Rob couldn't disagree.

"I told you."

They made it all the way upstairs and Dana still hadn't gotten through. Bishop held the door open for a nurse as she left the room.

"Thank you, Katie," he said to the young girl as he spotted Rob and Dana.

"What have you got?" He pointed to the bundle of papers under Rob's arms.

"A suspect," Rob said as Dana walked down the hall, her phone held up in the air, looking for a signal. He shook his head at the sight of her. "John Michael Reeves." Rob held up a picture to show him. "He's a former janitor at this very hospital."

"That's how he picked them out," Bishop said with a spark of realization.

"What's that?"

"I've been trying to figure it out all day. How did he choose the girls? Social media? Charities like Big Brothers? Nothing added up. He matches the BAU's profile perfectly."

Rob thought back to the bullet points he'd read earlier and recited them.

"Early to mid-thirties, menial job, organized. This guy has almost unlimited access to everything here and people see him as just part of the background. Invisible."

Bishop nodded along.

"He could have just checked the charts for girls that fit his preference and gotten all the information he needed."

Rob looked past Bishop and saw Dana still roaming up and down the hall looking for a signal.

"How's it going in there?" Rob asked.

"Slowly." Bishop looked at the closed door. "Get everything to HQ before your team makes any moves."

"Should we alert the media?"

"No. He's not going to kill them, but he may act erratically if he's stressed. We can't risk that."

Rob still had his eyes on Dana as she struggled with her phone.

"Got it," he said as he patted Bishop on the back. Rob waved to get Dana's attention.

"Hey! Just use the nurses' station phone."

Dana threw her head back in resignation and joined Rob.

"Why does every hospital... Never mind."

"Come on, they've got a phone right over here," Rob said. As they approached the tall desk, Rob saw the young nurse, Katie, on the phone. She spoke with a whisper, but there appeared to be an urgency in her eyes as Rob and Dana got closer.

"Gotta go," Katie said as she hung up. She straightened up and smiled at them. "Can I help you?"

Rob showed her his badge.

"Just need to use your phone."

She nodded quickly and put it up on the ledge for them. Dana held the receiver to her ear with her shoulder and held the switch down.

"How do I dial out?" she asked, but the nurse was already out of earshot. Rob pointed to a label above the keypad.

"Dial nine," he said. Rob shuffled around while Dana called in their findings. The young nurse went from room to room, writing her initials on various charts, but kept glancing at Dana as she did. Rob paid it no mind. She was likely on edge with all the cops and feds rushing around. Dana was finishing her call and stole Rob's attention back.

"Yep," she said into the phone. "Got it, Chief." She hung up and placed the phone back behind the barrier of the desk. Katie rushed back over and asked if there was anything else she could help with.

"No, thanks," Dana said.

"What's the plan?" Rob said.

"Gorman wants us to go check out his last known address. A house registered to his foster mother. It's not far from here and he's sending backup just in case."

"I'll drive," Rob said.

"No way, stunt man." Dana thanked the nurse again and they left. As the elevator door closed, Rob saw Katie smile at them and pick up the phone again.

- 9 -

The man had fallen asleep, face down in the photo album. The shrill and incessant ring of the telephone stirred him awake. He took a moment to adjust to his surroundings. The long night had taken its toll on him. He closed the book with gentle care and ran his hand over the leathery cover and ornate impression lined with gold inlay. The phone beckoned still and he shuffled toward it. He pulled the receiver from its hook and inhaled before answering.

"Hello?"

The voice on the other end was quiet and soft but filled with haste.

"Johnny, it's me."

"Me, who?"

"Katie. From work."

"Oh. Is something the matter?"

"Johnny, I'm worried about you."

"I'm doing fine. You worry too much."

"There's cops and FBI agents all over the place here."

His heart raced at her words.

"Do you know why they're there?"

"Haven't you seen the news, Johnny?"

He thumbed his nose. The smell in the old house had grown worse. He never noticed it much, but it was definitely getting stronger.

"I don't really have a television."

Katie sighed on the other end.

"Johnny, two little girls were kidnapped this morning and they've got two other ones they just found last night."

He rubbed his head as images of his sisters flashed in front of him.

"Sounds like they're looking for a real sicko, Katie."

"That's the problem, Johnny. I saw one of them walking around with your picture. Looks like they think you had something to do with it."

He did his best to control his breath. He felt the air well up in his chest, insistent on expulsion. He slowly inhaled to calm himself, but the stench of the house filled his nose. His heart pounded and the phone felt like a hot iron against his ear. He had to maintain his composure and not give himself away.

"That's crazy. Why would they think that?"

"I don't know, Johnny. Just tell me it's not true."

He wanted to tell her. She was the only person who even came close to understanding him. He wanted to lay it bare and unburden himself, but there was still so much to do and he couldn't be interrupted. He looked down the hall to the basement door and thought of the two little girls asleep down there. Still so much to do.

"Of course it's not true."

Katie sighed with some relief.

"Of course. Listen, Johnny, I can't talk much. They're headed my way. I just had to hear it from you. Gotta go," Katie said and hung up without pleasantry.

The man let the dam of panic burst as he hung the receiver back on its hook. He had so much to do. They would be on their way, though. He smashed his fist on the old wood table and it held its ground against him. A sting ran up his arm and he shook his hand at his side to relieve the pain. He gathered the photo albums and rushed out the back door. He loaded the rickety old car with everything he would need. Up and down the stairs, collecting what he needed. The noise of his haste stirred the girls from their slumber. The injection had lingering effects that kept them quiet and groggy, but their eyes followed him around as he scuttled about.

He had loaded all necessities and went to collect the girls. He nudged Sarah on the shoulder.

"Wake up. We have to go."

Her eyelids fluttered as she tried to keep her eyes on him.

"Are we going home now?"

"No, sweetie. We're going to have a party."

"What's that smell?"

"Never mind. Come on. Hurry."

"I want to go home now."

The man pulled away from her as urgency and impatience pulsed through his body.

"I told you, Sarah," he said as he turned and calmed himself but only for a moment. He grabbed a syringe from his desk and shouted as he approached her.

"You are home!"

Jessie gasped behind him as he plunged the needle in Sarah's arm. He turned to Jessie and pierced her skin as well. He stood straight and let the empty syringe fall from his fingers. He looked back and forth between them as they drifted off yet again.

"I'm your big brother," he whispered, "and I'm going to take care of you."

He carried the girls, one by one, up to the old car and laid them down gently in the trunk. He had lined it with blankets and pillows so they would not get hurt by bumps and the rough road. He eased the latch into place and pressed down to secure it before he got in and started the engine. He took one last minute to take a mental inventory. He tapped his fingers against the steering wheel as he tried to think. Had he forgotten anything? No. He was ready. He smacked the wheel with his palm and cursed the FBI for ruining his perfect plan. No. Not ruined. Only altered and displaced. He knew where they would go. Still away from it all. It would be just as good as his original plan. It would be better. It would be perfect.

He shifted into gear and drove off, checking around for any onlookers that may have spotted him. The houses were far enough apart and surrounded by trees that gave him privacy. Nobody had seen him. He drove toward the mountains. Not too slow, not too fast. Just a guy out for an afternoon ride. He whistled as he drove past the big houses. He spotted a black vehicle in his rear view. It slowed way back down the road and stopped in front of his house. He kept his pace and smiled as he watched them step out and walk toward the house. Though he was happy to escape, even by such a narrow margin, sadness came over him. He knew he could never go back there. Not after they found out what was inside.

- 10 -

Rob and Dana split up to circle the house. He took quiet steps and was careful not to be seen through the windows. He tried to peek in but a layer of grime on the panes of glass provided an obstructed view at best. He stepped over a scattering of old, dry sticks that had fallen from the trees. They snapped under his foot despite his best efforts to avoid them. He came to a small basement window. As he crouched down next to it, he saw that it had been blocked out from the inside by black drapes and taped up newspaper. Some overgrown and neglected shrubs stood at the corner of the house. Chips of the pale green paint had fallen off over time and rested atop the bush. He heard the crunch of footsteps from the back of the house. He figured it was Dana on her way around, but drew his gun to be safe. He didn't plan on getting shot again.

He crept around the corner, crouched like a predatory cat, ready to pounce. He and Dana spotted each other from opposite sides of the house. She used her fingers to signal to him. The back door was ajar and the gentle breeze made it knock against the frame. They crept with precise steps, one foot in front of the other, toward the steps that led up to the door. Dana pointed her weapon at the entrance, a silent request that Rob should take the lead and enter first. He nodded and took the lightest of steps up the wooden stairway. A strange smell wafted in the breeze; something Rob couldn't quite place.

He nudged the door further open with his toe. Its hinges creaked as it gaped open. He scanned the kitchen with his gun as he reached for his flashlight with his free hand. The shade of the trees and the grimy windows blocked out the afternoon sun. Dana followed him inside and they made sure to stay close together as they cleared the main floor. Rob whispered to Dana as he searched.

"What's that smell?" It was stronger and obviously coming from inside the house. Dana didn't say anything. She just held a finger to her lips to keep him quiet. Every step they took might as well have been an alarm going off as the floorboards creaked and cracked. Rob shone his light down a stairwell that led to the basement. A girl's shoe lay on a step about halfway down. He beckoned Dana over to show her and they went down.

The smell grew stronger as they descended. Rob bent low to see better and found nothing but an empty room. Two empty beds without blankets. A bare light bulb hung from the ceiling and he pulled the chain.

The beds were empty. The house was empty. Dana relaxed and sighed with frustration.

"They were here," she said.

"Looks like they left in a hurry," Rob said as he surveyed the mess around the makeshift bedroom. An odd assortment of items was spread out on a desk. Dana knelt down by the beds and held something up to the light.

"Marshall, look."

She passed him an empty syringe. Rob didn't need a lab tech to tell him what drug it once held. He set it down and covered his nose.

"Seriously, what is that smell?"

"It is stronger down here, isn't it?" Dana jutted her chin at a door under the stairs. This time, Rob aimed his gun to cover Dana as she took the lead. The handle squeaked as it turned and Dana swung the door open. Though he jumped at the gruesome sight, Rob couldn't bring himself to look away. A fog of cold air rushed out from the small storage space accompanied by a blast of the stench, the likes of which Rob had never had the displeasure of experiencing before, obviously the source of the odor. The skeletonized remains of a woman, judging by the tattered dress, sat upright in a chair. Bits of decayed skin clung to the cheekbones. Her teeth, still intact, seemed to smile from the jawbones. Clumps of hair and rotten skin lay on her lap and around her feet. The chilling scene, the stuff of nightmares, had frozen Rob as if he was the one in cold storage. Dana had lowered her gun, but Rob held his aloft. He'd seen horrible things in his short time as an FBI agent, but nothing like that. All the bodies he'd seen were fresh, as in recently deceased. They all looked like people, still fully formed for the most part. Rob finally felt his brain regain control of his body and lowered his weapon. Dana leaned over to inspect the remains.

"Well, this changes things."

Rob made a noise as he inhaled for the first time since the door opened. Dana looked away from the body and shook her head, not with malice or mocking, but concern.

"Marshall," she said. "Snap out of it."

Rob nodded himself back into coherence and holstered his weapon.

"Yeah, no, I'm good. Who do we suppose this is?"

Dana scratched her head with the muzzle of her gun.

"Hard to tell. Adult. Woman. His wife or girlfriend. Maybe his mother."

The stench overwhelmed Rob and he made a flimsy excuse.

"I'll go call it in."

Rob went upstairs — not too slowly, not too quickly — just to get away. He heard sirens in the distance. Their backup was on the way. Rob sauntered around the living room. Below him, he could feel the hum of the cooling unit. He paced the perimeter of the dark room and shone his light at the framed pictures. Old photographs. Why did all these guys have houses filled with old photographs? The sirens sounded closer. Rob was about to go outside and meet the approaching team when something on the wall caught his eye. A picture of a smiling woman. The smile was a forced one, practiced for posed photos. But it wasn't the smile that caught his attention. Rob noticed the dress she wore. The same dress that was draped over the decayed skeleton in the basement.

Rob went out to intercept the tactical squad and police officers that had arrived. The fresh air filled his nose and he breathed it in deep as he held his hands up to get the police to cancel their raid.

"Stand down," he said. "The house is empty."

Some of the cavalry looked relieved, others disappointed. Perhaps they had hoped the girls would be there. Maybe they were looking forward to some action. Rob used one of the radios to call in their findings and spoke loud enough that everyone could hear him. The looks on some of their faces were exactly what Rob must have looked like down in the basement. He had some of the officers come in with him and process the scene. The detectives arrived within minutes and spearheaded the evidence collection.

Despite the smell, Rob went back down to join Dana. They both looked around for any insight into the mind of Reeves. Another old photograph on the tiny dresser between the beds. Twin girls in matching navy blue dresses. The fabric matched the excess on the desk behind them. Their hair was cut to be the same.

He wondered if twins actually enjoyed looking alike or if deep down, they despised it. The photograph said it all. The missing girls were surrogates. Look-alikes to fill his needs. Reeves wanted desperately to recreate something from the past, but what? Rob stopped thinking about why he took them and focused on where they went.

"Dana," he said.

"Mmm hmm."

"This guy can't be far."

"What? He could be anywhere."

"Look around this place."

"I am."

"No, think about it. He's all set up here. He's got everything he needs. Seclusion, a holding area. The nearest neighbors wouldn't see or hear a thing. Why would he leave this place?"

"Reeves is clearly a disturbed individual."

"Disturbed but clearly ritualistic."

"We interrupted his perfect plan," Dana said. Rob shook his head. Something didn't add up.

"But how did he even know we were coming?"

As the words left his mouth, the phone rang upstairs. All the footsteps above them stopped and the creaking floors quieted. Rob ran up the stairs, two at a time, with Dana close behind him. Rob held a finger to his lips to keep everyone quiet and picked up the receiver. He held it off his ear so Dana could listen in, too. He cleared his throat before he answered.

"Hello?"

"Johnny, it's Katie again."

"Katie?"

"From work."

Rob covered the phone with his palm and whispered to Dana.

"Tell Bishop to get her." Dana went away to make the call. Rob could hear her instructing Bishop and he made himself known.

"Katie, this is Agent Marshall with the FBI. I want you to listen to me very carefully. Agent Bishop is going to ask you some questions. Do yourself a favor and don't make a big scene."

There was silence on the other end until Rob heard Bishop collect her and she hung up.

Rob called Dana over and they went outside. She stayed on the phone as Rob rushed toward the truck.

"We must have missed him by a few minutes, Dana." He looked up and down the long road. "He couldn't have gone that way," he said as he pointed the way they came. "He had to go away from us. Let's go."

Dana's eyes shot back and forth as she listened to Bishop and looked down the road.

"What about the scene, Rob?"

"Fuck the scene," he said. "We can just go catch this guy right now." He didn't wait for her to concur and hopped in. She took a look around the area and seemed satisfied that it was in good hands before she joined him.

Rob took off as she was still buckling her belt. He flipped on the lights and siren and sped along the road, toward the mountains. Dana hung up and Rob's phone rang. He fished it out of his pocket and handed it to Dana.

"If that's Gina, tell her I'll call back."

Dana looked at the screen.

"It's Gorman," she said and put the call on speaker. "Chief, you've got Marshall and Brown."

"Listen up, Lane got some Intel on Reeves. The body in the basement is likely Clara Reeves, John's foster mother. She owned the house. She took him in when he was just eleven and ended up adopting him herself."

The woman in the basement didn't interest Rob just then.

"What we do know about our guy?"

"His records are sealed so there's some red tape to get through."

"Red tape is gonna help this guy get away, Chief."

"We're working on it."

Dana took the chance to chime in.

"Did Clara Reeves own a vehicle?"

"An old yellow Lincoln Continental."

"Can we get an APB out on it?"

"Already in the works."

"Thanks, Chief. Keep us posted."

Rob sped along the road, over dips and bumps, until they came to a stop at an intersection. Five different routes splayed out before them, any of which Reeves could have taken. Rob slapped the dashboard in anger and turned on the police radio.

"See if we can get air support from LAPD," he said to Dana.

"It'll take too long," she said. "We should regroup at headquarters."

"For what, more talk?"

"We need more information. It's the only way we're going to save the girls."

"We were this close, Dana. We had him."

- 11 -

Every police car the John passed along the way made his neck tense up. He kept his composure, mindful not to look away too quickly or stare too long. It was dangerous for him to drive through the city, but time was of the essence. The coppers would be on the lookout for a yellow car if they'd done their homework. He calculated it as an acceptable risk since he'd painted the old Lincoln a nice shade of baby blue.

The man drove up the winding road that led through the Verdugo Mountains, north of the city. The houses were close together at first, spreading further and further apart the deeper he drove into the range. He hummed along to Sinatra on the oldies station and the sights and sounds filled him with ease. He was pleased with his new plan. It would be even better than last year's birthday. More authentic. His last sisters had grown too old and the new ones would be perfect.

The sun beat down and the cicadas buzzed as they basked in the heat. The familiar houses, though some had been remodeled, made him think of Sunday drives with his parents and sisters. They always argued who would get to sit up front with mom and dad and, ultimately, control the radio dials. The last drive they took together was the day before the party. The day before everything changed.

The Sinatra song ended and he turned the sound off, uninterested in hearing AM radio commercials. One of the girls must have woken and banged against the trunk from inside. He was glad the medicine had worn off, though. They were nearly there.

He passed by the old blue house, the last one before their destination. The young couple who owned it were sitting on rocking chairs on the big wrap-around front porch. They were not so young anymore. He casually waved to them as he drove by. A friendly gesture from a stranger passing through. The hustle of the city was far off from these parts. Close enough to get to, but at a comfortable distance. Away from it all, as they say. The last stretch before his old house felt like a million miles. It was all open spaces out this way, mountain peaks for a backdrop. Big backyards that just merged with the landscape. The houses were mere ornaments on the splendid terrain.

He slowed the car and turned onto the dirt driveway. No, not dirt. It was different now. He shook his head and refocused. It was the right house, but things were different. The shutters on the house had been torn off and replaced with big picture windows with wooden slat blinds to block the sun out. His mother always had luscious, heavy drapes. His heart pounded. The old carriage house was gone. A brick and mortar garage stood in its place at the end of the fancy driveway. Such desecration. The wooden steps and porch that once welcomed him home had fallen out of favor for a cold concrete number. The city had spread out like the virus it is and infected his childhood home.

He parked next to a silver Mercedes and shook his head at the vanity that ran through the property. He opened the trunk to help the girls out and found Sarah awake.

"We're here!" he said. Sarah held her hand up to block the light.

"Where are we?"

The man took a deep breath in through his nose.

"Breathe in that fresh air, girls." He helped Sarah out of the trunk and woke Jessie with a gentle nudge. "Come on. It's time for your party."

He held their hands as they shuffled to the backyard. They were still groggy from sleep. At the back of the house, as he might have guessed, the long picnic table was gone, too. He cracked his neck to relieve the stress of the changes made to his house and sat the girls down in the cushioned chairs around the glass and steel patio set. They slumped back in their seats and he opened the big umbrella up from the center of the table.

"Wait here, girls."

John fetched the food from the car and set out a nice lunch for them all. Sandwiches, vegetables, and fruit. There was soda and juice to drink. He brought the leftover cake from earlier in the day for dessert. Bees, flies, and other winged pests buzzed around the table and the weary girls would wave a lazy hand to shoo them away.

"Eat up," the man said to them. The girls nibbled at the small sandwiches he had made. After a few bites, all the color drained from Jessie's face and she convulsed from the midsection. She leaned over the arm of her chair and let it all heave out.

"Uh-oh," Sarah said. She looked at the man with worry in her eyes. The man tilted his head and made a pouty face.

"Oh, you poor thing. Not a worry. I'll get that all tidied up."

He finished cleaning and poured a cup of ginger ale for Jessie.

"This will calm your tummy," he said. He stroked her hair and thought, perhaps, he had given her too much medicine.

They finished their lunch and he proposed they run around and play before cake time.

"Don't forget your dolls," he said as he handed them over. The girls took cautious steps off the slate patio and into the grass, looking around at the fields and mountain peaks that surrounded them.

The man turned his chair to keep an eye on them and felt content. The voices of his aunts and uncles echoed in his ears. The smells from years ago filled his nose. It was perfect.

But it all turned from dream to nightmare, as perfection so often does. Off in the distance, from the foot of the hills across the field, walked a man. All

dressed in black and headed straight for
the house.

- 12 -

Rob and Dana arrived at the police station that served as headquarters for their investigation. They had to park at the back of the lot as news vans had taken up the front spaces. As they approached the front doors, Rob saw a podium set up with an array of microphones. The vultures with their press badges turned in unison when one of them spotted the two agents. A flurry of handheld recorders were thrust in their faces as they stutter-stepped their way through the ravenous crowd. They were asked for updates or comments. An onslaught of questions hurtled at them from all directions. It reminded Rob of the circus on his front lawn the day his own son went missing and it filled him with disgust. The media were usually helpful and cooperative when asked, but they always wanted more, more, and more. Rob held his arm out to clear a path and keep them at bay. Bright flashes from the mob cast erratic shadows, disorienting him. He kept on his path and didn't speak a word. He needed to remain professional and, if he spoke, he knew his mouth would betray him. Behind him, he heard Dana politely decline them.

"No. No comment at this time. No, not at this time. Thank you, no comment." They reached the doors and, though the reporters remained outside, the wave of sound flooded inside. Rob had to shake his head at the spectacle the case had become. They were under pressure, sure, but that wasn't it. The frenzy always got under his skin like a bad rash.

They headed back to where Gorman had set up shop. The open floor, earlier a typhoon of chaos, had settled to a dull roar as officers spoke with officers; detectives with detectives. The FBI factions had segregated themselves in the office spaces. The Behavioral Analysis Unit was next door to the CARD team.

Rob saw his boss, Gorman, in discussion with who he assumed was the chief of police. He carried himself like a politician more than a cop, dressed to the nines and an entourage of assistants at his back. Rob figured a place like Los Angeles would have a top cop more comfortable with speeches and public relations than being in an actual police station. Gorman looked like he was in full kiss-ass mode. The only thing missing was a camera they could smile at as they glad-handed each other. Rob breezed past the pair and into the CARD team's room. He flopped himself down in one of the supposedly ergonomic chairs and slid to a proper slouch. His shoulder flared up with a hot pain and he dug out some of the pills he got from the hospital. Benevides and Lane watched him as he settled.

"So," Rob said, "what are we working on?"

Lane spun her laptop around to show him the screen.

"We've been getting all we can on Reeves. Have a look."

Rob scanned through the utterly useless information scattered on the screen. Things they already knew. Things that wouldn't help find him.

"What about before he was put in foster care?"

Benevides looked out at the two chiefs.

"Gorman's still working on that."

Rob couldn't help but shake his head.

"Working real hard..." he said. Lane took her laptop back from Rob and tapped away at the keys as she spoke.

"They'll be addressing the media in a few minutes. We haven't been able to get in touch with a judge to unseal the juvenile records."

"Bishop get anything?" he asked.

Benevides nodded and checked his notes. He always kept a notebook. Probably a holdover from when he was a detective in Miami.

"The girls opened up to him," he said. "He kept them prisoner in that basement. Treated them like animals all year round. Except for one day. Every time their birthday came around, he was like a different person. He doted on them, made them cake, gave them presents. But then the next day, he'd go right back to playing warden. Fed them scraps and rotten leftovers. If they ever got out of line, he pumped them full of drugs. That was that. Year after year, that was their lives. Their birthday was the only thing they could look forward to."

"Christ," Dana said.

"Best we can figure," Benevides said, "is the girls got too old and they didn't fit the fantasy anymore. So he set them loose."

Lane opened a new file on her computer and pointed at the screen.

"The BAU gave us their profile," she said and read it out to them, but Rob had tuned it all out. He just stared at Gorman. He'd positioned himself to look like a hero if things turned out well, but just far enough away not to have a finger of blame pointed at him if the whole thing went sideways. Sickening. And smart.

Gorman and the police chief strutted away together, off to have their moment in front of the cameras. He wondered if they made arrangements for equal face time with the circus outside. The case was a public relations matter more than an investigation at this point. Rob wanted to change that and got up to leave.

"Dana, let's get out of here and actually do something."

She hoisted herself up again after she had just sat down.

"This is the part where I ask what, where, and why, and then you say something vague but I go along anyway to make sure you don't get killed, right?"

"Am I that predictable?"

The whole team looked at him and nodded. Rob shrugged and waved to beckon Dana to join him.

"I'll drive," he said.

They went out the back entrance to avoid the media and Rob's phone rang. Yet again, it was Gina. He sighed as he let it ring. Dana seemed put off by his dismissal.

"Can't you at least shoot her a text message? Maybe she saw you on TV with your arm in a sling and got worried."

"She's fine."

They strolled right past the press conference without notice and drove away. There was no breeze to relieve the heat of the sun as they were once again stuck in traffic. Rob thought about what Benevides had told them. For years, the families had to wonder what happened to their little girls. Alex was taken from him for nine months and it felt like an eternity. Dana kept looking over at Rob as if he was expected to say something.

"I give up, Marshall. Exactly where are we going?"

"I don't know."

"Very enlightening."

"There has got to be something we can do other than sit around at the station."

"Well, we can't just drive around."

"What about those juvenile records? Where would they keep those?"

"Social Services, I guess."

"Worth a shot," Rob said. "Let's go."

Dana looked out at the traffic lined up in front of them at a standstill.

"I've got news for you, Rob. We are going."

"Come on, hit the siren."

"It's not exactly an emergency."

"We're in LA. It's like the unofficial song of the city."

Rob maneuvered through the traffic as best he could, siren blaring and lights flashing. Only about half the drivers even bothered to pull over for them along the way. Dana got on the phone as they drove and tried to get a warrant to release the records. She attempted to reach multiple judges with no luck. They were all either out of the office or in session at court. Rob could sense Dana's frustration as they neared their destination. They arrived at the Social Services building and Rob barely waited for the truck to stop before he got out. Dana called out to him as she got out.

"Marshall, what do you think you're gonna do? You can't just waltz in there and raid their computers."

Rob stopped and waited for her. He was disappointed in her lack of urgency. She always followed the letter of the law and, sometimes, that wasn't the best way to get results. Just like back when Alex was taken, she had her protocols to follow.

"I can at least try," he said and held up his badge like it was an all access pass.

"For God's sake, Rob. Do you ever think about due process? Or how about the court case, ever think about that?"

"Fuck the court case," Rob said and kept walking. "That's the district attorney's problem. I'm gonna go solve this thing and show Gorman how you get results."

Dana stopped in the middle of the parking lot.

"So that's what all this headstrong crap is. You're just after that promotion."

"Oh, please."

"No. I can see it now." Dana shook her head as she stepped toward him. "Do you even care about getting those girls back home to their families? About locking this asshole up? Or is it all just a means to an end for you?"

Rob was furious and stood square to Dana as she stopped right in front of him.

"Tell me I'm wrong, Rob."

She wasn't wrong, though. Not wholly. He wanted to show what he was made of. Like a cornered animal, he hated Dana for calling him out like that.

"How dare you!"

"Let's say you go in there and break the law to catch a break. What if we catch Reeves and then he walks on some technicality? He could start over and do it all again to someone else."

"Just like the day I met you," Rob said with disgust in his voice. "You could have done more to find my son, but you're a slave to the rules."

Dana grabbed his shoulder and pressed her thumb against his bullet wound. He recoiled with a scream as the pain tore down his arm and across his back. She left him there in the parking lot, holding his shoulder, and walked back to the truck. Rob had crossed the line. She was there for him back then. The whole team was. He swallowed his pride and joined her.

They sat in the truck not speaking. They just stared at the dashboard, both with guilty gazes, both unwilling to break the silence. Finally, Rob straightened up with a deep breath, about to take the first step when Dana whipped her head around to face him. She hadn't used the time to calm down.

"If you ever speak to me like that again, you'll think I took it easy on you today."

Rob nodded and was about to apologize, but Dana had already moved on.

"We should go back to the house," she said. "There has to be something we missed in there."

"Good idea," Rob said and drove off.

They rode in relative quiet, save for the few phone calls Dana took to try and prod things along with the sealed records. The hum of the engine and sounds of the city provided the soundtrack for their drive to the secluded neighborhood that John Reeves called home. The thick trees blocked out the sun and made it feel a few degrees cooler than it did in the California sun. Rob and Dana walked with slow, purposeful steps around the outside of the house as the crime scene investigators and detectives rushed back forth all around them. The tool shed was empty except for some old gas containers and gardening implements that hadn't seen use in years. They shined their lights in every nook and cranny of the property before they headed inside. A burly police officer stood guard at the front steps and demanded identification before granting entry. Rob couldn't blame the guy. Even though they were first on the scene, there must have been a whirlwind of names and faces and badges zipping past the big cop that day.

Rob had seen enough of the basement and, frankly, didn't want another potential glimpse of the rotten corpse down there so they did a thorough check of the upstairs. Some of the detectives had bagged items that would yield DNA, just in case, and left them on the kitchen table.

Rob kept his badge in hand as he wandered through the house to curb the suspicion of the other officers. The bedrooms were as busy as the other rooms, crammed with not only people but a lifetime's worth of belongings that had been carefully given a place in the home. Nearly every inch of the walls served as a display for a framed photograph or homespun artwork. The carpet was mismatched throughout the house as was the paint. Nothing matched, but it all went together. The family photos painted a happy picture as Rob strolled the hallways. It reminded him of home. Since they'd gotten Alex back from those maniacs that took him, Gina took and hung up as many pictures as she could. The whole family, happy together. Just like it should be. The chatter around him struck a strong reminder that, right now, two families were incomplete and in the midst of a desperate nightmare. He could never know what the girls were feeling, but he knew all too well what hell the parents were in. He shook his head and brought his focus back to the job.

Rob found himself in front of a bookshelf in the living room. The higher shelves had kitschy trinkets that had been collected over years or handed down from past generations. A thin layer of dust adorned them like fallen snow. A complete encyclopedia set filled another slot on the shelf. Rob remembered the salesmen that would come around in the old days, door to door, to hawk their finely crafted, genuine leather editions and laughed at the memory. The other shelves held a mix of binders, paperback romances with cracked spines, and some big scrapbooks with homemade labels. One of the large books had no label and, judging by the lack of dust in comparison with the others, it had been put there recently. Rob grabbed some latex gloves and pulled it out to have a closer look. The thick pages were coated in plastic and were full of cut and pasted news articles. The paper had yellowed with time despite preservation efforts. They were set with meticulous care, one per page, as not to detract attention from one another. Rob flipped through the book and scanned the headlines.

Mass Murder. Tragedy. Verdugo Mountain Massacre. Lone Survivor. Sullivan Boy Exclusive.

Rob called out to his partner.

"Dana, come look at this."

"John Sullivan, the little boy who witnessed the slaughter of his entire family..." Dana trailed off and Rob nodded as she had come to the same realization he had.

"Looks like we won't need those records unsealed after all."

Dana dialed a number on her phone as Rob looked at more pages.

"Lane," she said, "it's Dana. Find everything you can on John Sullivan and the Verdugo Mountain Massacre."

- 13 -

Panic gripped John's heart as the stranger dressed in black approached the house. The sun sparkled off of something in his hand. A knife? Maybe a gun? It was all happening again. He should never have come here. He knew one day the stranger would return for him. The girls had stopped in the yard when they spotted him, too. John had to protect his sisters this time. He would not let the stranger hurt them again. He couldn't live through it again. The reporters, the cameras, the police, and so many questions. It was all too much. He took an instinctive step toward the tiny shed to evade the stranger. No, the stranger would not be permitted to carry out his wicked deed. He had to protect the family. He wouldn't be caught off guard, not like his father was. He was ready this time. He had prepared himself for the stranger's return. Everyone was counting on him this time and he would prevail. Then the reporters and cameras and police could bask in the glow of his heroics.

His grip found a sharp knife on the table and he set out to intercept the stranger.

"Hello?" the stranger called out. "Are you all right?"

John held his hand to his ear, almost in disbelief at what he thought he heard, and the stranger spoke again.

"I said, you ruined my life!"

John stopped dead still and nearly dropped his knife. He tightened his grip and with it every muscle in his body tensed. He felt momentarily frozen in place and felt his teeth grind. The stranger came ever closer. John couldn't see a weapon. It had to be hidden behind his back. He wasn't frozen, though. He sprung forward, past the girls. The stranger halted at the sudden movement and reached in his back pocket. He took a step backward as John raced toward him. John was at full speed now. The stranger pulled his hand from his back pocket and a flash of the sun beamed in John's eyes. Glass. No, it was metal. Likely a knife. The stranger turned to run and dropped what he held, but John overtook him with the prowess of a lioness hunting prey. He leapt and tackled the stranger. They tumbled to the ground and John sank his blade into the flesh of the stranger's thigh. He howled in pain and John turned the blade before he pulled it out. He wanted the stranger alive, but immobile. He needed answers. The knife poured a stream of thick blood from its tip and John heard the girls scream behind him. The distraction allowed the stranger to squirm and attempt to release himself from John's clutches. He took care of the stranger's other leg in the same way as he tried to crawl away.

"Please," the stranger begged, "don't kill me."

"That would be too lenient a punishment for what you've done to me."

He dragged the stranger by the arms, a streak of blood behind them in the dirt. John ordered the girls inside the house. The door was unlocked. The safety of life outside the city. The stranger moaned as he was lifted up the steps. John dropped his limp body on the tile floor of the kitchen and ran back outside to his car. He returned with a syringe and the girls huddled in the corner at the sight of it.

"You needn't worry," John said to them. "It's not for you."

He hovered over the stranger. He looked like he hadn't aged a day since the massacre. He had changed his face some. Plastic surgery was all too common these days, especially amidst the vanity that is Los Angeles. It didn't matter. He was, at last, face to face with the devil that had haunted his dreams all these years. The stranger looked up and spoke.

"Who are you? What do you want from me?"

"I'm nobody, thanks to you."

"What are you talking about?" the stranger seemed confused and weary. "I've never even seen you in my life."

"You took everything from me. My family, my youth, my history, and my future."

"No..." The stranger's eyes were barely open. The medicine cast its spell on him and John hovered over him like a predator waiting for its kill to stop twitching. John leaned his face down close to the monster he had felled.

"I'm nobody," he said in an eerie whisper. "And now, so are you."

- 14 -

Rob and Dana drove out towards the mountain. Lane and Benevides were on the speakerphone.

"Where are you two?" Rob asked.

"On our way," Lane said. "About ten minutes behind you." The two other agents gave a detailed account of what they had found.

"The Verdugo Mountain Massacre happened exactly nineteen years ago today," Lane said. "Gary Dunsmore shot and killed fourteen people, including members of the extended Sullivan family at a gathering in the small community north of the city."

Benevides came on to give some background.

"Dunsmore was a client of the patriarch, Louis Sullivan, at his law firm.

They worked in a bunch of different areas of law, but mainly criminal defense. Louis Sullivan represented Dunsmore in a workplace sexual harassment case, but walked away from the case before it got to trial."

"We looked at that case, too," Lane chimed in. "By the time Sullivan bailed, Dunsmore's name had been dragged through the mud. More and more women came forward with accusations. Sullivan never said why he backed out, at least not publicly. There was speculation that he had come across proof of Dunsmore's guilt and didn't want to have a loss on the law firm's exemplary record. It ended up making Dunsmore look worse, guilty or not. The day before the trial was set to begin, Dunsmore showed up at the Sullivan house in Verdugo. He was dressed in black combat gear and armed to the teeth. He shot and killed Louis Sullivan first. Then his partners from the firm who were visiting that day. The little boy, John Michael Sullivan, hid behind the shed and went unnoticed. Details after that are spotty since he was only ten back then. He was adopted by Linda Reeves and assumed her last name."

"My God," Dana said. "Ten years old and you watch your whole family get shot down."

Rob shook his head as he tried to make the connection.

"But why kidnap two girls and keep them prisoner for five years? Why not just go after the guy that did it?"

"Dunsmore killed himself just before police arrived. Reeves didn't have anyone to take it out on," Benevides said before Lane went on.

"The family gathering was for John's younger twin sisters. It was their eighth birthday party. Police found the him laying next to the girls in a state of shock."

Benevides came back on.

"Bishop figures that Linda's death triggered a psychotic break and Reeves kept her body hidden. Probably to keep collecting her disability payments. He's been surrounded by death his whole life and then he was all alone again. So he comes across two girls that reminded him of the twins and he's been trying to recreate the perfect birthday party for his dead sisters ever since."

Rob started to piece it all together.

"The girls in the hospital just got too old and he needed two new ones to continue his plan."

"You got it," Lane said. "Now that his lair has been disturbed, though, he's even more dangerous and unstable. Bishop is certain he went back to the house in the mountains. If he knows we're coming, there's no telling what he might do."

Benevides gave them a warning.

"No sirens," he said. "Don't even engage until we get there with the SWAT team."

"Copy that," Rob said.

Unexpectedly, Gorman's voice came on the other end.

"Don't be a hero, Marshall," he said. "I mean it."

Rob looked at Dana with surprise.

"Yes, sir. See you all there."

Dana hung up and looked at Rob.

"You're going to follow orders this time, right?"

She knew him too well.

- 15 -

John held the knife mere inches above the stranger's heart. With a simple push through the skin, he could kill him in an instant. Drugged and unaware, the stranger croaked out a restless moan. John looked into those glassy eyes, the gateway to the mind of his captive monster. Between the streaks of blood still on his blade, the sun sparkled in from the window. His breath was heavy as he straddled his downed prey. Long, heaving bursts of air in and out of his nose. He could smell the blood as it pooled around them. Pulsing slow and steady, in an ever expanding puddle of red against the white tiles of the kitchen floor.

He imagined himself, nearly twenty years ago. He was no longer the frightened little boy. The hunted had become the hunter. He felt his lips curl up in a smile. The blade shone against the sunlight again. He wiped it on his pant leg and held it up in front of his face. He was somebody again. He was a whole person. His eyes caught their own reflection and he saw something he hadn't seen since he was a small boy. The eyes of a killer. The eyes of a monster. The eyes of the stranger that took his father and mother; all his relatives and his dear little twin sisters. His sweet and innocent sisters who had never hurt anyone. The shell of a man who was nobody had finally become somebody. He was John Sullivan again, only different now. No longer was he a frightened child alone in the world, but a horrible devil, just like the stranger before him. This was what he was meant for. The reason he survived the carnage all those years ago. The reason he had to suffer his whole life up to this very moment. He was destined to reap justice for his slain family. He was reborn in that instant and his purpose was clear. John pressed his blade between two ribs and sunk it in. The stranger woke and strained against the pain, his lung punctured.

John was interrupted by a ringing phone in the other room and ran around the house, yanking out every phone line he could find. There was nobody else at home. The old country house was too different for him and it made his head hurt. Designer furniture, trendy artwork. No charm at all. Just cold and showy. Gray walls and monochrome rugs. Bland and soulless decor. It wasn't right. Had his memory betrayed him? Was it even the right house? No, this was the place. He shook away the doubt. The stranger must have changed it all on him just like he changed his face. Far too many things had changed, though. Those other girls had to be let go. They'd grown too old and started to get defiant. Their bodies had built up a tolerance to the drugs and he couldn't control them as easily. He only wanted things to be perfect again.

He glanced at the two girls cowered together in the corner of the kitchen as the expanding pool of blood crept closer and closer to them. The drug would stop the stranger's blood from clotting. He would soon be gone, but John wanted more than a slow fade. He had to take from the stranger what was taken from him.

"Girls," he said, "go sit on the couch now." They complied in silence and walked away. Their eyes never left him until they had stepped out of view. He heard the squeak of the leather sofa from the other room and knelt closer to the stranger. Bubbled and gurgling breath spewed from his bloody lips. John had seen enough trauma at his hospital job to know internal bleeding when he saw it. Time was short. John whispered in the stranger's ear.

"You took everything from me," he said. "Now I'll make you suffer for it."

The stranger rocked his head back and forth in denial. John was surprised by the stranger's defiance, so close to death as he was. He assumed he would beg or plead, maybe even ask forgiveness in a last-ditch attempt at repentance for his past sins. John tightened his grip as he readied the blade. The damp sweat of his hands proved problematic and he placed his palm over the butt of the handle, ready to plunge the knife in again. The stranger rocked his head again, his eyes wide with fright and realization of his inevitable fate. John basked in the moment and felt a true power rush through his body. He wished it could last forever. He lowered the sharp tip down and pressed against the red-stained shirt. Slowly, with a slight resistance against the flesh, his blade pierced the skin of the stranger's abdomen and he pushed it in slowly. John savored the feeling as a smile crept across his face. In that second, his mind flashed images of every gruesome detail from twenty years back. He imagined himself as the hero. A fantasy in which he anticipated the threat before anything bad happened. He would have rushed across the field and intercepted the stranger. He would have taken him down and sunk his knife into the black heart that beat inside his chest. He would have saved the day and nobody would dare try to hurt his family ever again.

John pressed his knife in further and the stranger groaned in pain. He heard the girls giggle from the other room. They were happy and playing a game together.

"Patty-cake, patty-cake, baker's man," they sang in unison. Their hands clapped along with the rhyme. John eased the blade out as slow as he sunk it in. He repeated the torturous process just above the stranger's collarbone. His paced heightened in tandem with his confidence. He was in complete control of the monster who had tormented him his whole life. The stranger managed to croak out an appeal.

"Please... don't," he said. "I'm not who you think I am."

John kept right on going as he replied.

"You killed my family twenty years ago. Right here at this very house."

The stranger moaned again as John slid the knife back out. He tried to lift his arm, but it flopped back down with a slap against the tile floor.

"Twenty years ago?" he said. "I was only eight..."

"You're a liar."

"My name is Kevin. I just bought this house a year ago when I moved here from Oregon."

John ignored him as if he wasn't even there. The stranger was trying to trick him, but he knew better. A trapped animal will do anything it can to survive. John held his knife up and sucked in a heavy breath. It was time. John rested the sharp tip of the knife against the fabric that covered his heart and the stranger finally begged.

"Please. It wasn't me. Please don't."

John enjoyed the eleventh-hour plea. The girls continued to clap out their rhythmic beat in the other room as they sang their song. All time seemed to stop just then and an intoxicating feeling of euphoria swept over him. He felt every pulse of blood race through his veins. John was, in that moment, a god of justice and righted wrongs.

The sensation was short-lived, though, as his ears caught a sound. It was far off. Outside, but coming closer. The howl of a siren. He didn't have much time left.

The police had found him. John released his anger and frustration with a shout so loud it startled the girls. They shrieked in unison, startled by the sudden outburst. John raised the knife high above his head, ready to plunge it down with a lifetime of fury behind him, but his arm froze in the air as the back door cracked and split. Light spilled in as it whipped against the drywall behind it.

"Freeze! FBI!"

- 16 -

Rob drove fast along the country road. It was all but deserted except the odd car out for a slow cruise in the afternoon sun. He passed by them with his emergency lights on to make sure the cops weren't called on him. He didn't want to losc thc element of surprise. Dana squirmed in her seat as she geared up in her bulletproof vest. She set up an in-ear radio for the both of them as well. In all the cases Rob had worked on, he'd never been in a potential hostage situation before. Dana had, though. She had told him once that nine times out of ten, it ends without violence. But that outlier, that one in ten as she said, is something that you will carry with you forever.

Dana switched the radios on and checked that they were working properly.

"All set," she said as she peered out at a mailbox on the side of the road. "Looks like we're almost there, better slow down so we don't miss it." Rob eased off the gas pedal and checked around the area. The mountains made the houses stand out like little models against a diorama backdrop. Ahead, the road bent and he took the turn with caution. The houses were spaced out erratically and he didn't want to happen upon their destination around the blind corner. He never trusted GPS outside of a major city. He checked the address on the next mailbox and, based on the numbering scheme of the houses they'd already passed, the next house would be the one they wanted.

The road now ran parallel along the mountain range and Rob spotted the house, a bright white speck in the distance. Dana pointed to a gathering of trees up the road a bit.

"Park it there," she said. Rob's pulse quickened as he pulled over. As an agent, this was new ground for him to break and he was going to have to rely on Dana's experience. His instructor at Quantico was right. You can train for a thousand lifetimes, but you're never really ready until you've been out there in the real world. He donned his own best and they tested their radios with normal speaking voice and whisper to make sure they could hear each other. The plan was to stick together, but they were prepared if they split up nonetheless.

Rob popped the magazine out of his Glock to make sure it was full; a habit he had developed over time. He slapped it back in with a click and pulled the slide to load the chamber. Dana did the same. Perhaps he picked it up from her.

They crossed the road at a slight jog, weapons at their sides, headed across the open field that led to the side of the house. There was a risk of detection as they approached. Rob took notice that the blinds were all closed shut, but they moved as quickly and quietly as they could. Dana stopped to crouch in the front corner of the house and Rob followed suit. She held a finger to her lips to signal silence then motioned for him to follow her around to the back of the property. The smell of fresh cut grass filled Rob's nose as they snuck around back, just out of sight under the windows. The wind whipped at them from across the open landscape and carried with it the freshness of the country air. It was a serene setting, but

Rob shuddered at the thought of what could be happening in that house. Sullivan was unhinged and about to be cornered.

One of his first cases with the team was unsuccessful. The missing boy was killed before they ever got on the case, but it rattled him for a long time. It rattled all of them. Then Dana, as if she had been listening to his thoughts, looked at him and whispered.

"Keep sharp, Marshall. If we play this right, it won't be that one in ten."

He nodded to agree and peeked his head around to see the backyard. His eyes darted around to take everything in as quick as possible. A garage, a picnic table, and some abandoned lunch. Near the end of the drive, a baby blue Lincoln. The same model they were after, but a different color. Sullivan had the forethought to paint it. A smeared line of dark red blood led from the edge of the concrete patio to the back steps. Or was it from the house and out toward the mountains? Whose blood was it? He turned back behind the shelter of the corner and pointed two fingers at his eyes to get Dana to have a look. She peered around and took everything in as quickly as he did. She looked skyward in pensive thought when she leaned back against the wall. It was already a bad situation and they both knew it.

Rob ran through all the possible scenarios in his head. Sullivan might have hurt the girls and dragged them inside or the current resident was the owner of the spilled blood. Either way, it was unlikely that the blood belonged to Sullivan. The girls couldn't have overpowered him. Even if the homeowner defended himself and neutralized Sullivan, why drag him inside the house? One thing was certain; John Sullivan was very dangerous right now.

Dana pointed at her eyes and motioned for Rob to go around the house. They had to try and get a visual on Sullivan. Rob went first and crept lower. His legs ached from the exertion as he crouched and stepped along, trying to be as quiet as possible. He rose slowly and stretched up on his toes. His heart pounded like a drum. If Sullivan spotted him, there was no telling what he would do. Rob carefully gripped the ledge of the window with just the tips of his fingers and was about to pull himself up to look in when he heard a sound in the distance. Police sirens.

He knelt back down and cursed the heavens. They had to act fast. The sound would be audible inside the house at any second. He and Dana exchanged glances, both running tactics through their minds. She darted past him with her hand held downward to keep him there. She sped around to the other side of the house to check another window. Rob heard her voice come through the radio in a whisper.

"I have a visual on the girls," Dana said. "They aren't hurt."

Rob felt a wave of relief wash over him. He whispered back to Dana.

"Copy that."

There was no doubt in his mind that some rookie got all fired up and was headed straight at them. There would be hell to pay, no matter what the outcome. The droning wail of the oncoming police car must have been heard inside. Rob's fear was confirmed when a scream bellowed out, right above his head. The tiny squeal of the startled girls sprung him into action. He looked at the staircase that led to the back entrance. Sullivan was just beyond that door. His body took over and he hurtled up the steps, his right foot already barreling at the space between the doorknob and deadbolt. The force burst the doorframe to pieces and he was inside, gun at the ready. The sun illuminated the room and he trained his sight on Sullivan, knife raised above a bloodied mess of a body on the floor.

"Freeze! FBI!"

Rob's finger, as if by instinct, found the trigger. But in that instant, Dana's words rang through his head.

It won't be that one in ten.

Sullivan had a look of shock on his face as he shielded his eyes from the sudden burst of daylight. Rob sprinted from the doorway toward him. He had dropped his gun and was upon his target as it bounced on the tile floor. His left hand gripped Sullivan's wrist to control the knife and he buried his shoulder in the bastard's chest. They crashed to the floor in a heap and Rob slammed Sullivan's wrist down against the hard white tile. The knife clanged out of his grip, just out of reach for both of them. Sullivan struggled and grasped at the blade before he rolled his weight back toward the fight. Rob was caught off guard and Sullivan was on top of him. They grabbed at each other's wrists in a frantic grappling match to try and gain control. Sullivan postured himself up, but slipped in the puddle of blood that had crept in around them. His weight crashed down on Rob and their heads collided.

Specks of white light danced in front of Rob's eyes as his head lolled to the side.

His eyelids fluttered to stave off slipping into unconsciousness and, as he lay there, one of the girls stepped into view from the other room. She looked drained and had dark circles around her eyes, but seemed otherwise unharmed. She looked at the two men fighting with surprise in her wide eyes and Rob felt himself weaken at the sight of her. He strained to keep Sullivan at bay as his brain recovered from the blow. Blood dripped from Sullivan's face into Rob's left eye and he clamped it shut, ignoring the salty sting. Sullivan's feet found purchase and he raised up again. Rob turned back to face him as he got a hand loose. He looked at the knife on the floor. It looked to be within reach, but his depth perception was weakened. Sullivan took notice as well and snatched it up before Rob could. The whole exchange lasted no more than mere seconds.

That was when Rob heard Dana's voice in his earpiece and from across the room.

"Drop the knife, John!"

Sullivan didn't even look back. His eyes just locked on Rob's chest.

In that split-second, Rob had his life flash before his eyes. Everything important, truly important, crossed his mind's eye and it was simple and beautiful. Just an image of Gina and Alex smiling at him and nothing else in the whole world mattered to him then.

A loud boom came from the doorway. Sullivan reared back and screamed in pain as the big kitchen knife slipped from his fingers. A spattering of blood and drywall pelted Rob in the face. The knife fell and sliced against Rob's abdomen.

Sullivan flopped down and clutched at his mangled hand, shouting in agony. Dana had disarmed him with an expert shot and it gave Rob enough of a jolt to buck his hips and get out from under him.

His trained instinct took over and he kicked the knife away as he handcuffed Sullivan within seconds, bloody paw and all. He clenched the cuffs tight around the wrists without mercy and leaned in close. Between Sullivan's shouts, Rob read him his rights.

Both Kayla and Emily looked in from the other room just beyond the carnage of the kitchen with a look on their faces that Rob would never forget. They weren't scared, nor were they relieved that police had saved the day. They both just looked on with bewilderment at the bloody scene. They would both get to go home to their families and sleep in their own beds again. But after today, neither of them would ever be the same innocent little girls they were before.

- 17 -

Rob watched as one of the LAPD officers put Sullivan in the back of the cruiser. The paramedics had patched his hand up and it was good enough until someone could sew him up in a more controlled environment. They weren't taking any chances with him. He kicked and screamed the whole way, rambling about some stranger. The owner of the house had been rushed off to the hospital. Nobody was sure if he would make it. He lost a lot of blood and probably had internal bleeding, too. Rob winced as the EMT worked on his knife wound. He had hardly noticed it inside the house. Now that the adrenaline had worn off, though, it stung like hell. She applied a gauze pad on top and lowered his shirt back down.

"Eight stitches to add to your collection," she said. Rob groaned as he was finally able to lower his arm.

"Thanks," he said as the technician cleaned up her things. Rob rubbed his sore shoulder and thought about what Gina would say. He always told her that she worried too much. He smiled and thought maybe she was right. With a gunshot and knife wound all in one day, he wouldn't be able to brush it off as no big deal.

Dana was with the girls. They sat together on the back bumper of another ambulance and drank juice boxes while the paramedics checked them over. They had latched on to Dana and she wasn't going to leave their sides. Their parents were on their way and would be there any minute.

Rob looked back at the police cruiser. Sullivan was still shouting but, with the windows up, he wasn't heard by anyone who didn't want to listen. Rob spotted Chief Gorman. He had arrived with Benevides and Lane, just behind the cop cars who had taken away the element of surprise. Their Captain was already on their case about the whole thing so Rob figured he'd let it go. Gorman marched around, getting information from the various higher-ups that were on the scene. The once quiet country house was a mess of flashing lights from ambulances and law enforcement vehicles.

The press hadn't heard wind of it yet, which made Rob happy when he saw yet another pair of cruisers pull up to the property. The officers got out and opened the door for the parents of the little girls. Their tear-stained faces and bloodshot eyes were all too familiar to Rob. It came with the territory. There were too many times when the team had to leave parents in that unsure state and move on. It was a harsh, bureaucratic reality that resources had to be used elsewhere. He remembered the feeling when his own son was kidnapped and the CARD team had been pulled off the case. It was absolute devastation. A kind of resignation that implied the worst possible outcome. He hated it every time they had to drop a case. Rob never forgot those people, though. He and Dana often brought the old case files along to go over them on the plane, just in case.

The faces of the parents searched around the area even though the officers led the way. Rob looked over to the ambulance and signaled to Dana with a nod of his head. She spotted the parents and leaned close to the girls to tell them who had arrived. She pointed through the maze of vehicles and cops. Their tired little faces filled with color and their darkened eyes filled with joy as their parents burst into tears at the sight of them. The pain in Rob's shoulder and abdomen melted away at that moment. All the hustle and chaos around him faded out and, when those families embraced, all the stitches and bullet wounds and promotions didn't matter at all.

Dana left her stoop and joined Rob.

"Never gets old, does it?"

Rob nodded in silent agreement.

"How are they?" he said.

"Physically, they're fine."

Rob knew what she meant. Alex had horrible nightmares for a solid year after he came back home. Therapy helped him through it and a return to normal life was easier when they were so young, but it would never leave them. These kids would carry this ordeal with them for the rest of their lives. Rob snapped out of it and looked at Dana. She was in her own world, too. Arms crossed, head tilted, and admiring the reunion before them.

"I never did thank you," Rob said. "That was one hell of a shot."

Dana smiled without breaking her gaze.

"Don't mention it."

"Well, thanks for everything today."

Rob looked around and took a deep breath of the mountain air. His phone buzzed in his pocket and it caught Dana's attention, too. They both looked at the screen and Dana gave him a playful punch on his good shoulder before she headed over to join Gorman. Rob stepped away to the open field at the back of the house and answered the call.

"Hello?"

Alex's excited voice came through the line.

"Daddy, it's me!"

"Hey, big guy! You know, I was just thinking about you. "

- 18 -

The jet cruised above the clouds, headed back east toward the night. Rob brought his attention back from the little window at his side and leaned out to look down the narrow aisle. In the seat closest to the cockpit, Gorman busied himself with the beginnings of what would be a mountain of paperwork. Rob had flouted a lot of the rules on this case in an effort to, admittedly, make himself look better. During the case, he told himself that he was just trying to find the girls, but deep down his motives were equally selfish. It took Dana to slap some sense into him.

Benevides leaned back in his seat, his oversized headphones pumping music into his ears so he could shut his brain off. Dana and Lane were behind Rob as usual. Their mundane chit-chat helped them unwind and Rob welcomed it, too. He stretched his legs out and turned around to join in. They talked until the sun was a specter in the distance behind them. Gorman came to the back to get some coffee and, on his way back, tapped Rob on the shoulder. He motioned for Rob to follow him to his seat. Dana raised an eyebrow as Rob got up. He had thought that Gorman would wait until they got back to Washington to chew him out. No sense in delaying the inevitable, he figured.

Rob sat across from Gorman and his neatly organized pile of papers and folders. He wanted to lay bare everything he had realized that day and started before Gorman could.

"Chief, rumor has it that you're transferring out and it should be no secret by now that I really wanted to take the lead, get this case solved, and show what I was made of."

Gorman thumbed at the files in front of him. He opened Rob's personnel folder and glanced up at him.

"I had you at the top of my list this morning, Marshall."

Rob knew there was more to that, but went on.

"I know I went out of line quite a bit today. I'm not looking for forgiveness or mercy. I can own that. But I want you to know that things changed for me today. This promotion, it's not what I got into the Bureau for. It's not me."

"You seemed pretty driven before," Gorman said. "Why the change of heart?"

"It took someone else to show me what's really important to me." Rob looked toward the back of the plane at Dana. "Out there in the field, helping those kids and their families, that's what I signed up for. I can see that now, thanks to Dana."

"Agent Brown," Gorman said with a curious tone. He picked up her folder and glanced over it.

"Absolutely, sir. She's the kind of person this team needs as a leader."

Gorman closed the folder and looked at Rob in silence for a moment before he spoke.

"What do you say we put today behind us and start fresh Monday morning?"

Rob had no intention of questioning the motives behind the free pass he was just handed and returned to his seat.

Exhaustion combined with the serenity of the night sky begged his eyes to close.

Before he drifted off, he heard Gorman beckon to Dana and she joined him at the front.

Over the next few months, the team had a string of successful cases under the leadership of Chief Dana Brown. Rob, along with the rest of the team, received multiple citations for bravery and they quickly garnered a reputation as the best CARD team in the country. Every time a family was reunited, it was more than enough for Rob, though. He turned down a number of lucrative transfers along the way. Some were because he and Gina didn't want to relocate, but that was a thin veil of an excuse. He wanted to stay with the best group of agents and the people he considered his extended family.

Sullivan or Reeves, whatever he was calling himself, was safely behind bars awaiting trial. Kevin Boyes, the homeowner that Sullivan had nearly stabbed to death, was on the mend. The doctors were able to stop the internal bleeding and everything else just needed time to heal. Sullivan's defense lawyer would likely argue insanity and a long, drawn out process would eventually see a sentence served in a mental health facility. It wasn't a question of guilt at this point. It was just a matter of punishment.

Thankfully, there were a couple of consecutive weeks when the team wasn't needed in the field. They revisited old cases and helped out at the academy, all while catching up on paperwork and spending their evenings at home instead of jetting around the country. Rob even got to do career day at Alex's school.

After another calm, peaceful day at the office, Rob drove home. He whistled along to a song he hadn't heard since high school. It was one of those one-hit wonder weekends and there were some forgotten gems playing that reminded him of his younger days. The sun was setting earlier and earlier as autumn marched on and Rob got home just as the orange streaks of light shone through the back window of the house, intersected by the tall trees that stood just beyond their fence.

Rob couldn't resist as he stepped through the doorway and bellowed out a hokey greeting.

"Honey, I'm home!"

Alex ran out of his room and hugged him. Gina wasn't far behind with an embrace of her own. They ate pizza and shared their daily news with each other. Rob and Gina were washing the dishes when she remembered something.

"Oh, some mail came for you today," she said. "I figured it was from the office so I didn't open it."

She dried her hands off and rummaged through the papers stacked up next to the microwave. Finally, she produced a manila envelope with no return address. Just Rob's name and address scrawled in nearly illegible lettering.

"Thanks, hon," Rob said and headed to the computer room. He couldn't explain why, but he stared at it for a minute or two. There was something odd about it, something he couldn't quite put his finger on. Curiosity eventually took over and he peeled up the adhesive closure. He peered inside and saw a single sheet. It was thicker than regular paper. He slid it out slowly until the full picture came into view.

It was a black and white picture that looked to be taken from a distance, like those old surveillance shots taken with a telephoto lens.

It was a picture of Rob on his front porch, dressed for work and heading out for the day. Gina was at the doorstep and they were waving goodbye to each other. Alex was propped in the window as he always was when Rob left, waving as well.

Rob looked around to make sure nobody was around to see the unnerving photo. Who would have taken it? And why send it to him? His mind raced through myriad possibilities. It could have been a nosy neighbor. Maybe some deranged fan of sorts that had seen him on TV during a case. He stared at it for what felt like a long time. He tried to envision where the photographer could have been to get the shot. Ground level, for sure. From the street, just down a bit. He picked up the envelope again. No names or addresses anywhere. No postmarks or stamps, either. It was hand delivered. He put it down to make sure he didn't damage any fingerprints on it.

He could hear Alex as he practiced his lines for the upcoming school play. Rob closed the door over so nobody wandered in. He looked around for something to use as a glove. The tissues on the desk would have to do. He examined the envelope again, looking for fibers or hairs that may have gotten stuck in the folds, but found nothing. He pinched the corners of the photograph and held it up in front of him. He turned it over and what he saw made him drop it face down on the desk. He stood there, staring at the reddish-orange writing smeared across the backing. His heart raced as he looked down at it. The yellow desk lamp reflected the light up at his face. He had seen enough blood to

know what it looked like when it dried
and there was no mistaking it this time.
He read it over and over in his head,
almost saying it out loud. Just one word
was written:
REVENGE

THE END

ABOUT THE AUTHOR

Brian Colborne is a Canadian author and family man. He has worked in the fields of wireless technology and telecom as well as the financial sector.
Scattered in were stints as a bass player and songwriter in rock and heavy metal bands
He lives with his amazing wife and two wonderful sons in London, Ontario where he grew up and hopes to stay for the rest of his life.
If you want to be the first to know when Brian releases a new book, please visit

http://www.bcolborne.com

and sign up to get an e-mail notification for new releases. Your e-mail will never be shared for any reason
Stay Connected

Website: http://www.bcolborne.com
Twitter: @bcolborne
Facebook: facebook.com/BriColAuthor